P9-BZR-499

THE FIREBIRD ROCKET

The launching of the Firebird Rocket is endangered when a famous rocket scientist disappears without a trace on his way to the Woomera Monitoring Station in Australia. Assigned to the case, Fenton Hardy tells his sons he needs their help. And Frank and Joe must turn down a request that they find the missing son of a prominent senator.

The search for the scientist begins at the Princeton Space Laboratory, where the boys realize they are being hunted by an unknown adversary. Clues lead them to Australia, and again they are followed.

Then suddenly their lives are in danger!

Someone in an automobile tries to run them over; and, later, at dockside, a heavy cargo bale falls and just misses them. Disregarding the danger and warnings of worse to come, the boys follow the trail to a cattle station in the Australian Outback.

With courage, wit, and clever detective work, the young detectives begin to close in on the enemy, only to discover that the tables have been turned. Captured by their cunning adversaries, the Hardys face certain death!

Will they escape? Will the Firebird Rocket ever be launched? Read this exciting mystery about Frank and Joe's most difficult case.

"Your nitwit contraption smashed my hen house."

Hardy Boys Mystery Stories

THE
FIREBIRD
ROCKET

BY

FRANKLIN W. DIXON

NEW YORK
GROSSET & DUNLAP
Publishers
A FILMWAYS COMPANY

Printed in the United States of America

CONTENTS

THE
FIREBIRD
ROCKET

CHAPTER I

A Frantic Warning

FRANK and Joe Hardy were performing a chemical test in the laboratory over their garage. The boys were checking out a clue for their father, famous private detective Fenton Hardy.

Frank held a test tube up to the light. In it was a dark-colored solution soaked from a torn piece of cloth Mr. Hardy had sent from the Space Flight Center in Florida, where he was working on a new top-secret case.

"If Dad's hunch is right," said Frank, "that cloth was stained with the invisible dye he uses to trap suspects."

Joe nodded. "The methyl test will tell us."

He picked up a plastic bottle labeled METHYL YELLOW. Unscrewing the cap, he tilted the bottle until a trickle fell into the solution.

Pufff! A burst of acrid vapor shot up into the boys' faces. They staggered back, clutching their

1

throats! Frank dropped the test tube, which smashed, and the bottle fell from Joe's nerveless fingers, clattering onto the wooden floor! The two boys rubbed their eyes, fought for breath, and felt giddy.

"The bottle!" Joe croaked. "It contains the wrong chemical!"

Desperately Frank groped about on the floor till his fingers closed over the plastic container, which was still oozing a wisp of vapor. He managed to screw the cap back on. Joe opened the window, and they collapsed on the sill.

Fresh air poured into the lab, dispersing the fumes and clearing their heads.

"That stuff was liquid tear gas, or I'm a monkey's uncle!" Joe exclaimed.

Frank examined the bottle. "It's supposed to be methyl yellow," he declared. "That's what the label says."

"Somebody switched it!"

"That's possible. But who? And why?"

"Let's talk to the guy at the chemistry shop who sold us the bottle," Joe suggested, always eager for a mystery.

Joe Hardy was blond and seventeen. His dark-haired brother, Frank, was a year older.

As they were clearing up the mess from the broken test tube, the Hardys heard the doorbell, which was wired to ring in the garage as well as the house.

"Aunt Gertrude will answer it," said Joe.

"She can't. She went out shopping with Mom," Frank told him. "We'd better go see who it is."

Hurrying out of the garage, they went through the house and opened the front door. The caller was a well-dressed, portly man, clutching an ivory-headed cane. He peered at the boys through gold-rimmed pince-nez, which he held in place on his nose with thumb and forefinger.

His gesture called their attention to the ring he was wearing. It was set with a huge red ruby.

"Is this the Hardy house?" he inquired in a deep booming voice.

"Yes, sir," Frank replied.

"I'm Oliver Ponsley," the man announced. "I would like to consult Fenton Hardy on an urgent matter."

"Dad's away on a case right now, but would you care to come in and tell us about it?" Frank said politely. "As soon as we hear from him, we can give him your message."

"Thank you. I would appreciate a chance to explain my problem."

Frank led the way into the living room. Their visitor settled himself on the sofa, which groaned under his weight, and clasped his hands over his ivory-headed cane. Frank and Joe sat down in easy chairs and waited for him to speak.

"You boys often assist your father on his cases, do you not?" Ponsley inquired, sizing them up with a shrewd glance.

"That's right, sir," Frank replied.

"And we've solved a few mysteries on our own," Joe added, grinning modestly.

"So I've heard. Well, then, perhaps you can help me with this one, at least until your father returns."

"We'll be glad to do whatever we can, sir."

"Fine! My problem is this—a young man named Michael Moran has disappeared, and he must be found. Quickly!"

"Have you notified the police, Mr. Ponsley?" Frank asked. "They should be able to help you on a missing persons case."

"Not on this one," Ponsley retorted sharply. "We can't risk the publicity. Michael Moran is the son of Senator Jeff Moran!"

He reached into his pocket and produced an old snapshot, which he handed to Frank. The Hardys saw a clean-cut youth, not much older than Frank, holding a baseball bat on his shoulder.

"That's the last photograph of Michael before he left home," Ponsley told them. "He's been gone for over a year now."

"A *year?* Good night! Hasn't his family tried to locate him at all?" Joe asked.

"No. They felt he wanted to go away and think things out for himself, and that he'd come back when he was ready."

"Then why are they looking for him now?"

"Michael used to work for the Mid-County Bank. As you may have heard, the bank was recently broken into and robbed."

"Gosh, yes. I remember hearing about that on the news!" Joe exclaimed.

"The next day, the police caught the two crooks who pulled the job," Frank recalled.

"That's right." Ponsley nodded. "What you may not know is that the culprits are now trying to incriminate Mike Moran."

"How come?"

"The bank's alarm system was tampered with, which convinced the FBI that the robbers had inside help. So now those two scoundrels are saying it was Mike who gave them information on the wiring of the alarm system."

"Is there anything to support their accusation?" Frank asked.

"Mike studied electrical engineering before he quit college to work at the bank. And a bank employe named Thurbow remembered that Mike showed some interest in the alarm system while he was there."

"That doesn't prove anything," said Joe.

"Certainly not!" Oliver Ponsley boomed. "So far, the FBI has made no official charge against Mike, but his family is very upset, especially since Senator Moran is running for reelection. A scandal could wreck his political campaign. He's sure Mike is innocent, and wants him to come home and clear his name."

"Mr. Ponsley, how are you involved?" Joe asked.

"I'm on Senator Moran's staff and a friend of

the family's. I want to prevent any bad publicity before the news leaks out. That's why I came to see your father."

"Tell me," Frank said, "when and where was Mike last seen?"

"Leaving the bank one day last February. But he never arrived home that day."

"Has he written?"

"Yes, a number of postcards from Chicago. The last one came about three months ago, saying he was leaving the country. After that—silence."

"Any other clues?" Joe asked.

"Just one." Ponsley slipped the ring from his finger and held it up to the light so the boys could see it better. Sunshine slanting in through the window seemed to bathe the room in the gem's lustrous red glow.

"Michael always admired this stone," Ponsley said. "He was fascinated by rubies, so his parents bought him one as big as mine and had it mounted in the same kind of setting. Find a ring like this, and you'll find Mike Moran."

The Hardy boys examined the gem and felt sure they could easily spot a duplicate.

"Now then," said Ponsley, slipping the ring back on his finger, "I want you to get on the case right away. Fly to Chicago tomorrow and see if you can pick up Michael Moran's trail. Make your first report to me by the end of next week. Speed is essential!"

"But we can't leave town right now," Frank

"Find a ring like this, and you'll find Mike Moran."

said. "We're waiting for a phone call from our father. He may need us to help him with his own case."

"We'll let you know as soon as we're in touch with him," Joe added.

"Hmph." Frowning, Ponsley rose to his feet and adjusted his pince-nez. "Very well. If that's the best you can do, I'll just have to wait. You can call me at this number."

He handed Frank his business card and the boys escorted him to the door. They watched him lumber down the steps, squeeze behind the wheel of an expensive car, and drive off.

Frank and Joe returned to the living room.

"How about that ruby?" Frank enthused.

"Big as a pigeon's egg!" Joe said. "Boy, that stone must be worth a bundle!"

"Say, could thieves have gotten to Mike Moran?" Frank said suddenly. "Maybe they did him in for his ring!"

The two boys exchanged worried looks. Joe felt cold chills prickle up and down his spine.

"A ruby that size would sure attract crooks!" he agreed. "I wonder——"

He broke off at the sound of brakes screeching out in the street. Tires grated harshly against the curb in front of their house, and a car jolted to a stop. Its door opened and slammed shut. Someone raced up the steps and pounded on the door.

"Open up!" a man's voice shouted. "You Hardy boys are in danger! You may be killed!"

CHAPTER II

The Runaway Rocket

"Who the dickens is that?" Joe blurted.

"Search me, but he sounds pretty worked up!"

The doorknob rattled violently, and the thumping continued. Then their caller began ringing the bell.

"Take it easy! We're coming!" Frank yelled.

He yanked open the door. The man outside tumbled in and had some trouble regaining his balance.

"It's Mr. Oakes from the chemistry shop!" Joe exclaimed, recognizing his face.

The man was gasping. He stuck his hand into his pocket and pulled out a long plastic bottle. The label read METHYL YELLOW.

"My assistant made a terrible mistake," Oakes said, panting. "He put the wrong label on a bottle of liquid tear gas and sold it to you as methyl yellow. This is what he should have given you. If you use that other stuff in the wrong kind of chemical experiment, it could even blow up in your faces!"

"We know. We found out the hard way," said Frank. "We already had an accident."

"Great Scott! Was anyone hurt?" Oakes inquired anxiously.

"No, luckily we reacted as soon as we inhaled the fumes, and Joe got a window open fast."

"Thank goodness!" The man sighed with relief. "My store phone's out of order, so I hopped in the car and drove here the minute I discovered what Bob had done. You both have my deepest apologies. I'm terribly sorry."

"That's all right, Mr. Oakes," Joe said. "We were just about to come back to your place and find out what happened."

"A mistake—a dreadful mistake! Would you please give me that wrong bottle now?"

"Sure," Joe said. "I'll go get it." He took the methyl yellow out to the laboratory over the garage and returned with the liquid tear gas.

"We supply this stuff to various security guards around town," Oakes explained. "In fact, one of them came into my shop to get some just before I told Bob to fill your order. I suppose that's how the mix-up occurred."

After repeating his apology, the manager of the shop left with the dangerous chemical.

"Well, that solves one mystery," Frank said as he shut the front door. "Now we can concentrate on the Mike Moran case."

"Unless Dad needs us," Joe reminded him. "But listen. Suppose we do get a chance to look for that guy. How would we trace him in Chicago?"

"Good question. For one thing, we'd have to find out more about him—what his interests are, how he spends his spare time—stuff like that."

Frank broke off as the telephone rang. Joe hurried to pick it up, heard his father's voice, and gestured to Frank to come and listen in.

"Dad, where are you calling from?" he asked.

"The Space Flight Center in Florida," Fenton Hardy replied. "This case is turning out to be even tougher than I feared."

"Can you tell us anything about it?" Frank put in.

"Not on the phone. The investigation's being conducted under airtight security."

"We goofed on testing that scrap of cloth you sent us," Joe said. He told his father about the accident in the lab.

"That's all right. No harm done," said Mr. Hardy. "I identified the wearer by means of a polygraph test. I had him figured as a prime suspect in this case, but he cleared himself. Now I've got another job for you, at Princeton."

"You mean Princeton University?" Frank queried. "In New Jersey?"

"Yes. I want you and Joe to go there tomorrow morning. Talk to Professor Arthur Young at the Aerospace Laboratory. He'll clue you in on the case, and I hope he'll give you a lead to work on. Report to me after you see Professor Young."

"Dad, how do we get in touch with you?"

"You can reach me through a hot line to the Space Flight Center. The number is the Center's initials followed by the first four digits—SFC-1234. Got it?"

"Got it," Frank said.

Mr. Hardy's voice became tense. "Be careful," he warned. "This job is too important for any slips. NASA is involved. An international incident could be in the making."

"We'll be careful," his sons promised, then Frank told his father about the visit by Oliver Ponsley.

"He wants us to find Mike Moran."

"My case has priority," Mr. Hardy replied. "After we've cracked it, you can look for young Moran. So long." He hung up.

Joe replaced the phone and the boys began to talk about their trip to Princeton.

"The home of the Princeton tiger!" Joe said with enthusiasm. "Wow! Maybe we'll get a chance to see some of their athletic teams work out."

"I think we'd better just stick to the Aerospace Lab," Frank said. "We're on a case, remember? I wonder what Professor Young knows about Dad's investigation. Maybe somebody stole a missile!"

"Yeah, sure." Joe grinned. "Like maybe a crook slipped an interplanetary rocket up his sleeve and walked out unnoticed. If you ask me——"

He was interrupted by a series of loud reports in the street. A clanking sound drew near.

Frank grinned. "Chet Morton's coming."

Joe peered out the window at the approaching jalopy. "Looks like he's got the whole gang with him. Let's go see what they're up to!"

As the Hardys grabbed their jackets and ran outside, Chet's fire-engine-red car pulled up to the curb. Its roly-poly, freckle-faced driver applied the squeaky brakes and brought his car to a jolting halt that threw his passengers forward, then bounced them back in their seats.

"Should we call a doctor?" Joe inquired. "Or are all of you still in one piece?"

"Wait'll we check," said Biff Hooper, a husky six-footer. He was crowded into the back seat with Chet's pretty sister Iola and Tony Prito.

"No broken bones—yet," Tony reported. "The question is, will we be able to walk away from this moving wreck?"

"What I'm worried about is my back," groaned Phil Cohen, who was sitting up front beside Chet. "I think I slipped a disk when we stopped."

Frank laughed at the driver's indignant look. "What's that you were telling us, Chet, about your rebuilt shocks and the smooth suspension you were engineering on this job?"

"So it's got a few bugs." The stout youth shrugged. "I notice that doesn't stop these wise guys from thumbing a ride in my racer whenever they need a lift. You'll have to admit it's really sharp looking!"

"Pedestrians call it the *Red Menace*," Phil wisecracked.

The car's body metal had a worn, battered look but gleamed with a fresh coat of paint.

"Not bad for an old heap," Joe said, grinning. "When are you going to install a refrigerator?"

"Hey, that's an idea!" Chet said, snapping his fingers.

The Hardys' plump pal had helped them on many investigations. Even though he preferred food to danger, Chet never let Frank and Joe down when they were in a tight spot.

"Hop in, you two. We're wasting time!" he went on. "We can talk about food supplies later. Right now we're on our way to Bayport Meadow."

"What's going on there?" Frank asked.

"The most exciting scientific event of the century!" Chet exclaimed. "Up, up, and away! Don't miss it."

"Chet just finished his rocket," Iola confided. "He can't wait to try it out. It's in the trunk."

Laughing, Frank and Joe crowded into the car, practically sitting on their friends' laps. By now they were used to Chet's mania for new hobbies. His latest was rockets, and he had been working on one in his basement for weeks. He intended to enter it in a national high-school science contest.

The jalopy sagged under the extra weight but began to move. Chet drove it noisily through Bayport and headed for the meadow outside of town, while the others chatted and joked about the contest.

Joe had managed to squeeze into a place next to Iola. He usually dated her when the gang went to picnics or dances.

"Chet just might win," Iola told him. "He's really worked hard on this project."

"We'll all be cheering him on," Joe promised.

In a few minutes they reached the meadow, a large open area covered with dry brown grass. The soil was still slightly frozen from the winter's cold.

Chet parked and they all got out and checked the area to make sure no one was in the way of the test.

"Looks like you've got a clear firing range," Tony observed.

"As long as he aims straight," said Frank.

"Don't worry," Chet boasted confidently. "I've designed a foolproof steering system."

He opened the car trunk and lifted out his rocket. It was a two foot long cylinder with a pointed nose and tail fins. For a launching pad, Chet stuck two pipes in the ground, mounted a cradle on them, and placed the rocket in it. The

missile tilted at an angle with its upper end pointing skyward. Then Chet attached a control wire
with a switch at one end.

At last the tubby teen-ager stepped back
proudly to survey his handiwork. "Ah! Ready for
the countdown!"

"Man, that looks like a space probe to the
planet Mars!" Frank joked admiringly.

"Powerful enough to carry an astronaut to the
moon," Joe suggested.

"Any astronaut but Chet," said Biff. "With a
payload that heavy, even a Saturn rocket would
never get into orbit."

"Quiet, you guys!" Chet commanded. "The
Morton Moon Grazer is about to be launched.
My electrical igniter will do the trick. Here goes!"

He pressed a remote-control switch. There were
a flash and loud report, followed by a burst of
smoke. The rocket shuddered, left its cradle, and
shot high in the air. Chet's friends were impressed
and burst into applause.

Chet bowed. "It'll land at the far end of the
meadow," he predicted.

They all shaded their eyes and watched. Suddenly the missile began to wobble and veer off
course.

"Oh, oh! It's looping over to the right!" Joe
blurted.

The rocket appeared to be zooming down beyond the strip of woods fringing the meadowlands.

"There are farms on the other side of those trees!" cried Biff.

"What happened to your foolproof steering system?" Frank inquired.

Chet gulped and turned pale. "S-S-Something must have gone wrong!"

"No argument there. Come on! We'd better find out where your Moon Grazer lands!"

The boys and Iola ran around the edge of the meadow and headed through the stand of trees.

"Must've come down on Old Man Jessup's farm!" Phil guessed. "Boy, that guy's a real crab!"

Chet shuddered. It took them several minutes to cover the distance, and he was puffing and panting anxiously by the time they approached Jessup's farmyard. He turned even paler as the loud squawks of frightened chickens with an angry bellowing voice reached their ears from the other side of the barn.

"Oh gosh!" Chet exclaimed. "Sounds like we're in real trouble!"

"What do you mean *we?*" said Biff.

The words were hardly out of his mouth when the barnyard noises were drowned by the shrill hoo-haw of an approaching police siren!

CHAPTER III

The Blow-Up

A SCENE of wild confusion greeted the teen-agers' eyes as they rounded the barn. Feathers were flying as white Leghorns and Rhode Island reds hopped, cackled, and fluttered about the yard. Chet's rocket had smashed their chicken coop.

Enoch Jessup, a gaunt, bushy-browed man in overalls, was shouting orders to his farmhand, who was trying to round up the frightened fowls and calm them down by scattering feed.

Just as Jessup's glance fell on the young people, a police car with flashing lights screeched to a halt near the farmhouse. A burly man in a brass-buttoned uniform jumped out and strode toward the scene of the disaster.

"Oh, brother! It's Police Chief Collig himself!" muttered Tony Prito.

"What's going on here?" Collig demanded.

"You've got eyes! What does it look like?"

18

Jessup retorted. "These young scamps just wrecked my chicken coop with their blame-fool contraption! Scared the wits out of my best laying hens!"

Turning to the high-schoolers, he growled, "Which one of you's responsible for this outrage?"

"W-W-We weren't aiming at your chicken coop, Mr. Jessup," Chet stammered. "It was j-j-just an accident. . . . I mean, that is . . . well, I—I guess *I'm* sort of responsible."

"*Sort* of responsible, my foot! Your nitwit contraption smashed my henhouse, didn't it?" Shaking his finger in Chet's face, Enoch Jessup proceeded to bawl out the trembling youth.

"All right. All right! Take it easy," Chief Collig cut in. "We got a CB call from some motorist who saw you kids about to fire a rocket. Good thing I grabbed a squad car and came myself. I might've known you'd be at the bottom of this mess, Chet Morton. You and your harebrained hobbies!"

"Actually, Chet made the rocket for a high-school science competition, Chief," Frank Hardy spoke up. "I know the test went wrong, but he's worked hard on this project. I think he deserves credit for making a model that flew as well as this one did. After all, our country *needs* rocket engineers, and they have to start somewhere."

"Tell you what, sir," Joe added. "If Mr. Jessup won't press charges, we'll all pitch in and repair his chicken coop. We'll even help out with a few chores."

"Sounds fair enough," Collig agreed. "What do you say, Enoch?"

The farmer's scowl relaxed. "Why not? Makes more sense than wasting time in court."

Biff Hooper borrowed Chet's car keys and hurried off to get some fresh lumber, while the others cleaned up the debris from the wrecked coop. Luckily the coop had broken the missile's fall, so that the rocket itself was not much damaged.

"Boy, you Hardys really saved my neck," Chet said as they drove back to Bayport.

"Forget it. It was fun," Joe said.

"Think you can still enter your rocket in the competition?" Frank asked their chubby pal.

"Sure. I can make repairs tonight and turn it in tomorrow morning."

Although spring vacation had started, Mr. Palmer, the science teacher, had promised to be on hand at the high school to receive last-minute entries.

Frank and Joe found their mother and aunt just back from the supermarket. Aunt Gertrude was their father's sister.

"Where have you boys been?" she demanded tartly.

"Watching an unidentified flying object, Aunt Gertrude," Joe told her with a grin.

"What's *that* supposed to mean, young man?"

Her eyes flickered suspiciously over her two nephews.

The tall, sharp-tongued spinster was extremely fond of Frank and Joe and secretly longed to take a hand in their detective work, although she could seldom bring herself to admit it openly.

"Chet fired a homemade rocket," Frank said, and he described the crash landing.

"Good heavens! I'm glad no one was hurt," Mrs. Hardy exclaimed.

Aunt Gertrude sniffed. "That boy Chet needs a firm hand."

"Someone like you to help fire his rockets?" Joe teased.

"He could do worse," Gertrude Hardy snapped. "Apparently you two didn't help him steer it right."

The boys laughed, and Frank said, "Score one for Aunt G.!"

He told them about Oliver Ponsley's visit and their father's call. "We have to go to Princeton first thing in the morning," Frank added.

"Oh dear," his mother said. "I hope you're not going to get involved in anything dangerous." Mrs. Hardy, an attractive woman, worried whenever her husband and sons took a new case.

"Well, what's dangerous about going to a university?" Aunt Gertrude scoffed. "Might learn a thing or two there at Princeton, as long as they don't start playing any foolish college pranks."

"We won't," Joe promised, chuckling.

"You're going alone?" Mrs. Hardy asked, still a bit concerned.

"We were," Frank replied, "but now that you mention it, we might ask Chet to come along."

"Hey, good idea!" Joe said.

He rushed to the phone and called their over-weight buddy. Chet was delighted at the suggestion and agreed at once to accompany them.

"Pack an overnight bag," Joe advised. "We may have to stay a day or two."

"That's okay with me," Chet said. "I was just thinking it might be a good idea to stay out of sight the next few days. Chief Collig will probably have every cop in town breathing down my neck for a while."

Joe then called Mr. Ponsley and told him that they could not start searching for Mike Moran until they knew more about what was expected from them in their father's case. Ponsley agreed to the delay. "Call me as soon as you know more," he added.

Early next morning, the Hardys got into their sleek yellow sports coupe and picked up Chet Morton. Then they headed for Princeton. Threading their way through traffic, they reached the highway, where Frank stepped on the gas and kept the car whizzing along at the speed limit. Once the rush hour was over, they made good time under the brilliant sunshine.

"Get your rocket fixed, Chet?" Joe inquired.

"You bet. Handed it in just in time. I think I've really got a chance to win."

"I sure hope so. We'll keep our fingers crossed."

At a fork in the road, Frank turned onto Route 206 and soon they saw signs indicating that Princeton lay straight ahead. When they ran into Nassau Street, they knew they were at their destination. Shops lined one side of the famous Princeton thoroughfare, and university buildings occupied the opposite side.

"Now I know why it's called Ivy League," Chet quipped. "Look at the ivy on the dorms!"

"I wonder where the Aerospace Lab is," Frank said. He stopped for a red light near a couple of high stone gates flanked by iron railings. Beyond the lawn they could see Nassau Hall, the main building of the campus. Its slender tower rose toward the sky and was topped by a weathervane.

A student carrying a couple of books under his arm started to cross the street with the light. Joe leaned out the window and asked him the way to the Aerospace Lab.

"Go down Nassau Street and turn right onto Washington Road," was the reply. "The lab is near the football stadium."

Frank followed the directions. They passed the psychology and biology departments, and arrived at a science complex, where Chet spotted a sign reading: PRINCETON AEROSPACE LABORATORY.

Frank parked and the young detectives went in.

They found themselves in a rotunda, where a model of a Saturn rocket stood upright in the middle of the floor. Around the walls behind glass were exhibits of dramatic moments in the history of space exploration.

Chet pointed to one of them. "The astronauts on the moon!" he said.

"And there's Skylab in orbit!" Joe exclaimed.

"And Telstar!" Frank marveled. "They bounce signals off it out in space, and the signals are picked up by TV systems around the world!"

A guard approached and inquired what they wanted. When Frank explained their mission, he escorted them down the hall to a door bearing the nameplate: PROFESSOR ARTHUR YOUNG. The guard knocked and went in. A moment later he returned and announced that Professor Young would see them.

They entered a study lined with books, graphs, mathematical equations, and blowups of major rocket launchings. The professor rose from his swivel chair and shook hands with the visitors. After introductions were made, he made a motion indicating that they take three chairs near his desk, and sat down again. He was tall, thin, and slightly bald. He looked intently at the boys as he tamped tobacco into his pipe and lit it.

"Your father phoned me and told me you were on your way," he said with a smile. "I'm very glad to see you and your friend. We need fast action."

"Professor, what is the problem?" Frank asked in a puzzled tone.

"How much do you know about the case that has developed here at the lab?" Young countered.

"Nothing," Joe admitted.

"Well, I'll give you all the information I have. First let me show you around the place, so you get an idea of what we're doing. Then you'll see what we're up against and why we need your assistance."

He led them out of his office and through the building. "Everyone here is devoted to the exploration of space," Young commented. "This lab is one of the best in the world when it comes to interplanetary probes and the study of the solar system."

The group passed a lecture hall, a library, two seminar rooms, and several offices belonging to famous scientists. Then they arrived at the lab itself, a maze of rooms in which experts were carrying out experiments on everything from liquid fuels to the problems of weightlessness in outer space.

"Boy, this sure beats Bayport High!" Chet exclaimed. "I could make myself a real rocket here. Maybe I'll apply for a job after I win the state science competition."

Young laughed. "Glad to have you aboard,

Chet. Just be sure you get clearance from the Space Flight Center when the time comes. You'll have to be okayed down there because we work for NASA. What we discover goes on the drawing boards at the Center."

"No wonder Dad said the case was hush-hush," Frank put in. "This lab must be filled with top-secret stuff."

Young became solemn. "That's the whole point of the investigation you're undertaking."

They arrived at a room where a youth was working at a modified atomic reactor. Young introduced him as Smoky Rinaldo, a senior at Princeton University.

"Smoky can show you around from here on," the professor said. "When you've seen enough of the lab, meet me back at my office and we'll discuss your assignment."

He walked off and Smoky informed the visitors that he was doing research for a term paper.

"I'm into rockets, myself," Chet spoke up. "Fact is, I've got my own missile."

Frank chuckled. "You almost didn't. It flew straight—straight to earth."

"What are you talking about?" Smoky asked.

"Oh, nothing," Chet said hastily. "Why don't you show us the rest of the lab? I can't wait to see it."

The young people wandered through the last row of rooms, which were assigned to scientists experimenting with the shape of nose cones and tail fins for partly developed rockets.

Suddenly a movement caught Frank's attention. Looking out of the corner of his eye, he noticed a man behind them. He was tall and lanky and wore a black beard and tinted glasses.

Frank paused before a blow-up of a Saturn rocket. Joe and Chet joined him. The man stopped at a workbench and furtively glanced at them.

"I think we've got a shadow," the older Hardy informed Joe and Chet in an undertone.

Joe traced the curved line of a nose cone with his finger, pretending to be interested in it. "Are you sure?" he asked.

"No. It could be a coincidence. Let's go on and keep an eye on him."

Joe turned as they walked farther, catching a glimpse of the man. "Beard with glasses?" he asked.

"Right."

Smoky was slightly ahead of the group, explaining the interesting features of the lab. When they left the last room and walked back to where they had started, Chet asked, "Who's that guy with the beard over there?"

Smoky turned around to look. "I've no idea. Matter of fact, I've never seen him before."

The man obviously realized that the boys had noticed him, and instead of following them farther, he entered a door with the sign OFFICIAL PERSONNEL ONLY.

"He must be on the staff here," Smoky went on. "Would you like to see the reactor I'm working on? The interior is hot enough to handle uranium."

They walked over to the instrument. "We can't see the interior," Joe pointed out.

"That's because it's running," Smoky said. "Just follow me, and you'll find out what's in there." He led the way to a diagram on the wall representing a slice through the reactor from top to bottom.

"This is how the machine is put together," the student explained. "The core in the center marked A is where the uranium goes. The letter B stands for the pressure vessel, and C is the casing. These tubes extending from the core to the top are the fuel——"

A loud sputtering noise broke out. Red sparks flashed through the air around them. Chet turned pale and shouted, "The reactor's going to explode!"

CHAPTER IV

A Strange Disappearance

CHET dived to the floor, crawled under a workbench, turned around on his hands and knees, and stared at the other three. Frank, Joe, and Smoky remained standing.

"You guys want to get blown up?" Chet quavered.

"False alarm, Chet," Smoky said.

"How do you know?" Chet demanded.

"Because that wasn't the atomic reactor," Smoky explained. "It has a failsafe protection. If anything goes wrong, the motor shuts off automatically. And besides, this is a modified reactor. It doesn't have enough power for an atomic explosion."

A man in overalls came over. He was wearing a plastic eyeshield and carrying a blowtorch. "Sorry about that," he apologized. "I'm working on a wire coil with this torch. The coil's too soft for the flame, and that's the reason for the noise and sparks."

"That's okay," Smoky said. "Don't worry about it."

As the man walked off again, Chet crawled out from under the workbench and got to his feet. He looked embarrassed. "Guess I overreacted," he said sheepishly.

Frank soothed his feelings. "It's better than taking chances. Well, we've seen the lab. Let's report to Professor Young and find out about our assignment."

The Bayport youths left Smoky Rinaldo tinkering with the heat shields on the atomic reactor. They rejoined the professor, who shuffled some papers, placed them on the desk, and leaned back in his swivel chair.

"How do you like the Aerospace Lab?" he inquired genially.

"We like it fine, Professor," Frank declared, "except for one thing."

"What's that?"

"We were being followed." Frank told him about the man who seemed to be shadowing them through the lab.

Young frowned. "I've never seen anyone who matches that description, but I'll try to find out who he is. The lab is strictly off limits to unauthorized personnel."

He ordered through the intercom an immediate search of the premises. Then he turned back to his visitors. "Now," he said, "let me tell you about the mystery."

The boys leaned forward in their chairs, eager to hear every word.

"It concerns Dr. Adrian Jenson," Young went on. "You may have heard of him."

"The rocket scientist," Joe said. "He's been working on space probes ever since the astronauts landed on the moon."

"And he won a prize for his math on trajectories," Frank added. "The path of reentry from outer space into the earth's atmosphere."

Young smiled. "You know your rocketry," he complimented them. "Well, Dr. Jenson and I have been working on a revolutionary new engine powered by nuclear energy. We call it the Firebird, and it's due for a test flight in a couple of weeks. Dr. Jenson flew to Australia three days ago to follow the flight of the Firebird at the Woomera Monitoring Station."

"Australia?" Chet spoke up. "Why there?"

"When a rocket is fired into orbit from our Space Flight Center, its path over the Southern Hemisphere is followed at tracking stations south of the equator. Woomera is one of the best of these installations. We are cooperating closely with the Australian government in monitoring our missiles, and our people go there frequently."

"But why the mystery?" Joe asked.

"Dr. Jenson never got to Woomera. He hasn't been heard of since he left Princeton!"

Frank let out a low whistle. "Did he actually get on the plane?"

"Yes. We checked with the airlines. He arrived in Sydney and picked up his luggage. There the trail ends. We also searched his desk for clues, but found nothing."

"And you've notified the Australian police?" Joe asked.

"We did that immediately and they've been working on it ever since. However, both we and NASA wanted a top-flight investigator assigned to the case at this end—especially since there were indications that the plotters had been after him in this country. Our project's top-secret, so the investigation has had to be kept under wraps, and your father seems the ideal man to handle it. But so far we have no real clue to Dr. Jenson's whereabouts."

"Maybe enemy agents kidnapped him!" Chet exploded. "Maybe they're brainwashing him!"

"That's possible," Young admitted. "The Firebird Rocket is classified. Dr. Jenson and I are the only scientists who know the secret of the nuclear engine. If enemy agents kidnapped him, he may have revealed the secret. A foreign power could be building a Firebird right now!"

Frank said, "You mentioned that someone had been after Dr. Jenson in this country."

Professor Young nodded. "A neighbor noticed a car with Florida plates parked outside his house after he left. And the police discovered that his home had been broken into and ransacked. Also, telephone company records show that a call was made from there that same night to a pay phone in Florida near the Space Flight Center."

"So that's why Dad's been concentrating on the case down in Florida!" Joe said.

"Exactly. But he wanted all aspects of the case covered and decided his sons could handle the investigation here at the Aerospace Lab. So here you are."

"And we've brought Chet," Frank said. "He's helped us many times before and is reliable."

"That's fine," Young said. "I trust your judgment."

Chet grinned and said he would do his best to help the Hardys crack the case.

The professor continued. "Your task is to investigate all possible leads at the lab and see if you can find the clue you need to solve the mystery while your father does the same at the Space Flight Center. I have some information that might help you."

"Oh?" Frank asked. "What is it?"

Young's answer surprised him. "Jenson and I received a warning letter and threatening phone calls. Here, I'll show you."

He reached into a drawer and took out an envelope. Removing the letter, he handed it to Frank. Joe and Chet craned their necks to see it. The message was crudely pieced together from words out of a newspaper.

It said: *Kill the Firebird or else!*

"Someone's trying to sabotage your rocket!" Joe exclaimed. "They don't want it to be launched."

"That's right, and whoever wrote the letter means business."

"Professor," Frank said, "do you realize that you may be in great danger yourself?"

"Everyone here is aware of that. I have been assigned a personal bodyguard, without whom I do not leave the building. I don't want you to worry about me. Just find Dr. Jenson!"

Frank was about to say something when he heard a noise outside the door.

"An eavesdropper!" Frank thought. Leaping out of his chair, he strode to the door and swung it wide open.

Smoky Rinaldo was standing there!

"Hi," Frank said. "Are you interested in our conference?"

Smoky looked surprised. "I didn't know a conference was going on in Professor Young's office. When I heard voices, I stopped momentarily to see if I should come in or not." Glancing past Frank, he addressed Young. "I can't tell if the fuel is getting hot enough. Would you mind checking it when you have a chance?"

"I'll be right along, Smoky," the professor promised. Then he said to the boys, "I'll phone the Nassau Club and make arrangements for you to stay there while you're in Princeton. It's on Mercer Street."

Young made the reservations, then went with Smoky to the atomic reactor while Frank, Joe, and Chet drove to the Nassau Club. The driveway curved in a semicircle past the steps leading up to the front door of the stately building.

Frank parked the car. "Do you think Smoky was eavesdropping?" he asked as the boys got out.

"I'm inclined to think he's honest," Joe said. "But we'll keep an eye on him."

The boys entered the building and went to the front office to see about their room. Frank inquired while Joe and Chet looked around.

A hallway led through the first floor to a coatroom at the rear. Members of the club were seated in the reading room to the left, scanning the latest newspapers and magazines. Two portraits hung on the opposite wall, flanking the entrance to the main dining room.

"I wonder who those old geezers are," Chet whispered to Joe.

The younger Hardy walked closer, surveyed the inscriptions under the portraits, and came back. "They're two presidents of the United States," he said. "Woodrow Wilson and Grover Cleveland."

Frank strode out of the office and announced that they were set for the night. The three drove to the rear of the club and left the car in the parking lot. Walking toward the back door, they examined the building, which had plenty of corners and angles, tilting roofs and high eaves.

"The club would make a good haunted house,"

Joe suggested. "All we need is a spooky face at the window. Frank! There he is!"

"Who?" Frank asked, glancing in the direction his brother had indicated.

"The guy from the lab!" Joe gasped. "He was right there, looking out that window. The fellow with the tinted glasses!"

"I don't see him now," Frank stated, "but let's go inside and see if we can catch him!"

The boys hurried up the wooden steps and through the coatroom door. Seeing nobody, they hastened down the hallway into the reading room, through the dining room, and to the front door.

A footfall on the carpet made them whirl. Their shadow was trying to tiptoe down the stairs to the basement!

The boys rushed after him. As they reached the bottom of the stairs, they saw him run into the bar. By the time they got there, he was exiting by another door.

The pursuers went pell-mell up the stairs to the first floor, and then to the second floor, where Chet was too exhausted to go any farther. He sat on the top step and watched the Hardys race along the corridor to where the man was climbing out the window. The fugitive slid down the fire escape to an alley at the bottom, and hurried around the corner into Nassau Street.

When Frank and Joe reached the spot, the man had vanished!

CHAPTER V

Night Visitor

"No SIGN of him," Joe said, looking up and down the street. "He could be anywhere by now."

Frank nodded glumly. "You're right. We lost him."

The boys returned to the club and picked up Chet, then went to their room. It overlooked the alley and had a fire escape under the window.

"Good," Chet declared when he noticed the exit. "We can get out of here in a hurry if we're cornered by crooks. Say, how about chow? I haven't eaten since breakfast. I might faint."

"If you do, you'll shake up the club," Joe quipped. "It wasn't built for your weight."

Chet looked pained, but Frank came to his rescue. "I'm with you, Chet. It's dinnertime anyway."

The boys freshened up a bit, then went to the dining room. After giving the waiter their order,

Chet leaned back in his chair. "Well, Hardys," he grinned, "do you have a plan for solving the big mystery yet?"

"We're working on it," Joe said, sipping water from his glass.

"I think Jenson was kidnapped by a foreign power," Chet declared.

"Maybe he *worked* for a foreign power and left on his own," Joe put in.

"You mean as a spy?" Chet asked.

Joe nodded. "Perhaps he developed the Firebird Rocket and sold the secret to someone else."

Frank shook his head. "But why would he wait until the United States finished building the missile? I think he would have given away the secret earlier and stolen the plans in order to prevent us from completing the project."

Chet nodded. "I'm with Frank. The spy angle doesn't seem to fit in this case. Jenson was probably kidnapped."

"So where do we start with our work?" Joe wanted to know.

"We interview all the people at the lab," Frank said. "Let's hope somebody there will be able to give us a line on that bearded creep."

The boys discussed their strategy during dinner, and after they had dessert, Chet suggested that they go for a walk to clear their heads.

"I have a better idea," Joe said. "I noticed a sign saying that there's dancing after dinner. Why don't we listen to the music for a while?"

"Oh, good," Chet said. "I'm all for it."

A combo was playing in the lounge, and couples edged onto the dance floor. The boys sat down and before long Joe noticed three attractive girls standing nearby.

"Hey, what say we meet those young ladies over there?" he said.

"Sounds great," Frank agreed. "I'll invite them to our table." He got up and soon returned with the girls in tow.

"Hi," said the pretty blond right behind Frank. "I'm Hedy Hollweg. My friends are Pat Morrison and Jane Linski."

The boys introduced themselves and asked the girls to dance. Frank paired off with Hedy, Joe with Pat, and Chet asked Jane. After a while, they went back to the table, and animated conversation followed.

"We're freshmen at Princeton," Hedy said, "and are studying American literature. What are you doing here? I haven't noticed you on campus."

"Detective work!" Chet boomed. "I've solved a lot of cases with the help of the Hardys!"

Frank and Joe grinned. They were used to having Chet brag a little, especially in front of girls.

The coeds were intrigued. They bombarded the boys with questions about crime investigation.

"You must be here on an important case," Jane surmised.

Chet opened his mouth but Frank kicked his foot under the table as a signal to keep quiet about

Dr. Jenson. Joe changed the subject. "How do you girls like Princeton?"

"It's great!" Hedy said. "I'm glad they let coeds in."

Pat nodded vigorously. "This is one thing Women's Lib did for us. Princeton used to be for men only. But no more!"

"Personally, I wouldn't want to go to a school that excludes girls," Chet said, eying Jane appreciatively. He smiled at her. "Would you like to dance?"

The young people had a fun-filled evening, and when they finally said good-by to each other, the Bayporters thanked the girls for their pleasant company. Then Hedy, Pat, and Jane went to their dorm while the Hardys and Chet walked up to their room. Soon they were fast asleep.

A sudden noise woke Joe in the middle of the night. It came from the alley below their room. Throwing off his blanket, he got out of bed and padded silently to the window.

A pebble landed squarely on the pane. Joe peered over the sill into the darkness. He could barely see a figure on the ground below, throwing another pebble, and another.

Joe pushed the window open. "Hey, what do you want?" he whispered loudly.

"Joe! It's me, Smoky. I've got something for you!" was the reply.

"Okay, come up the fire escape," Joe said.

As Smoky climbed up the rungs of the ladder, Joe roused Frank and Chet. "We have a visitor," he told them. "It's Smoky."

"At this time of night?" mumbled Chet, who was still foggy with sleep.

"Strange time for a visit, all right," Joe agreed.

Smoky clambered in through the open window.

"What's wrong with the front door?" Frank grumbled.

"They lock the place up at night," Smoky explained, "and I didn't want to cause a disturbance."

"There's also the telephone," Chet pointed out.

"I know. But I didn't want to call because I have something to show you. I——"

"How did you know this was our room?" Frank interrupted.

"It was the only vacant one before you came," Smoky answered. "There was no other place for them to put you in."

"Smoky, I think you're crazy. Do you know what time it is?" Joe asked.

"Hey, don't get mad. I'm trying to help you!"

"Why couldn't it wait till morning?"

"Because I've got to get some sleep. I've worked in the lab till now and I have an exam at noon. By the time I would be able to call you, you'd be gone."

"All right. What have you got?" Frank asked.

Smoky withdrew a sheet from his pocket and

held it up for them to read. "Look at this!" he said.

A row of words had been cut out of a magazine and glued onto the paper, just as in the threatening note Professor Young had received. It read: *The Firebird will never fly!*

Frank, Joe, and Chet were flabbergasted by the message, which seemed to leap at them from the paper.

"Where did you get this?" Frank asked Smoky.

"It was under the blotter on Dr. Jenson's desk," the boy replied. "He keeps memos there. As I told you, I worked late on the reactor, and I needed to clear up a problem about the power transmission. I thought Dr. Jenson might have left a memo on it, since we talked about it recently. So I looked under the blotter and found this paper instead."

"Any idea how it got there?" Frank inquired.

"None. But I know that Dr. Jenson's missing and figured you're investigating. I couldn't help hearing that much when you thought I was eavesdropping in the corridor. I decided I'd better get this message to you pronto. I'll let Professor Young know about it in the morning."

"Thanks for your trouble," said Frank. "This could be important."

"Professor Young told us Jenson's desk was searched for clues when he disappeared," Joe said. "How come it didn't turn up then?"

"Must've been put under his blotter after that,"

"Strange time for a visit," Joe said.

Frank guessed. He shot a questioning glance at their visitor, waiting to hear his comment.

Smoky shrugged. "It could easily have been overlooked, because it was between a couple of memos. Well, I'd better be going. I have to get some rest or I'll flunk my exam tomorrow."

The boy jumped on the windowsill and swiveled his legs onto the fire escape. He climbed down into the alley and seconds later vanished behind the buildings.

Frank placed the puzzling message on the table under the light of the lamp and the boys studied the warning.

"What do you make of it?" Frank asked his two companions.

"The way it reads," Chet declared, "this could be a threat or just a straight message."

"Why cut out words to send someone a message?" Frank objected. "Why not just write it?"

"To avoid having your own writing recognized."

"Sure, but *whose* own writing?" said Frank. "Are you saying Jenson himself is a phony or a traitor?"

"Well, he must be," Chet argued, "if this is his work."

"Yeah. If! That's the question," said Joe.

"There's no way to tell. If you ask me, our first problem is, How did this get under Jenson's blotter after he disappeared?"

Frank glanced at his brother. "You think Smoky's lying?"

"Let's just say we have no reason to trust him so far."

"Maybe not. On the other hand, the message could have been overlooked, as he says."

"That's right," Chet added. "Jenson may have put it under his blotter and forgotten about it. Perhaps he didn't take the warning seriously."

"Boy, the situation looks serious now," Chet said. "If NASA goes ahead with the Firebird launching, it may be curtains for both Young and Jenson."

"For all we know," Joe warned, "it may have been curtains for Dr. Jenson already!"

CHAPTER VI

A Ghostly Hand

CHET gulped. There was silence for a moment.

Then Frank said, "We don't have much time to solve this case. Professor Young said the Firebird will be launched in a couple of weeks."

"From the Space Flight Center," Joe added. "Maybe Dad's onto something down there. Let's call him in the morning and find out."

The boys went back to sleep and were up bright and early. After breakfast they found the maid cleaning their room, which prevented them from using the phone. They decided to use the club phone in the basement.

Frank and Joe squeezed into the booth and shut the door, while Chet stood guard outside in case any suspicious character tried to listen in. Joe dialed SFC-1234, the hot-line number Mr. Hardy had given them for top-secret phone calls.

A woman's voice answered. "This is Space

Flight Center Control," she said crisply. "Please identify yourself and the party you wish to speak to."

"Frank and Joe Hardy," Joe said. "We'd like to speak to Fenton Hardy."

"Oh, yes. I've been alerted that you have clearance. But Mr. Hardy isn't here."

"Can you tell us when he'll be back?" Joe asked.

"Sorry, but I don't know. Mr. Hardy wasn't in yesterday, either, and he hasn't phoned. Would you like to leave a message for him?"

"Yes. Please tell him to call us at the Aerospace Lab or at the Nassau Club in Princeton as soon as possible."

Leaving the phone booth, the Hardys told Chet they had failed to reach Mr. Hardy.

"Where do you suppose he's gone?" said Chet.

Frank shrugged. "He may be following up an outside clue or keeping someone under surveillance. Maybe that's why he hasn't had a chance to phone."

"So what do we do now?" Chet asked.

"Let's go over to the lab and start talking to people," Joe said.

"Okay, but how about stopping at the library on the way?" Frank suggested. "I'd like to bone up a little on Australia. When Professor Young was telling us about Woomera yesterday, I realized how little I know about that whole continent."

"Same here," said Joe. "I guess we could all do with a quick fill-in on the scene down under. Who knows, it might even suggest another angle on the case to us!"

The three set out across the campus, passing students and professors on the way.

The university library was a stone building, three stories high. At the desk inside, Frank asked where they could find books about Australia. "On C Floor," an assistant told him. "Three stories down. You can take the stairs or the elevator."

"I don't know about you," Chet declared, "but I'll ride."

The Hardys followed him into the elevator, and Frank pressed the button. The doors closed, and they descended to the bottom floor, where a wall chart guided them to the left. Following the numbers that marked the shelves, they came to the section on Australia.

Each of the boys grabbed an armful of books, which he carried to a large circular table. They sat down and began to turn the pages, flipping through to the chapters and illustrations that interested them. Frank concentrated on geography and history, Joe and Chet on the people.

"I'm going to see if I can find something specific on Woomera," Joe said finally and stood up. He returned his stack of books to their places. Then he scanned those on the shelf beneath. As he reached for one, a ghostly hand appeared from the opposite side! It clamped around Joe's wrist and held tight!

Startled, the younger Hardy boy pushed a big volume out of the way with his free hand and looked through the opening. A young man grinned at him.

"Smoky Rinaldo!" Joe exploded.

"I couldn't resist it," Smoky said. "I'm a great practical joker, you know."

"Some joke," Joe grumbled. "You scared me half to death."

"I didn't mean to," Smoky said. "Sorry."

"What are you doing here anyway?" Joe asked. "I thought you wanted to get enough sleep to be fresh for your exam?"

"I woke up early so I came here to do some research. By the way, you're being watched."

"What?"

Smoky jerked a thumb in the direction behind Joe, who whirled around in time to spot an indistinct figure sneaking furtively between the stacks.

"I didn't get a good look at him," Smoky said, "but he seemed to be eavesdropping on you before, when you all sat at the table."

"I'm going after him!" Joe decided. "Want to come?"

"Sure thing."

Smoky and Joe met at the end of the stack. There was no time to alert Frank and Chet, since the man was hastening toward the exit.

Joe saw a ray of light reflected by tinted glasses. It was the man who had been shadowing them at the lab! He darted into the elevator and pushed the button. Joe and Smoky ran after him. He glowered savagely as they drew near, and then the elevator doors closed in their faces. The boys ran around to the stairs and took two steps at a time to the main floor, where they almost bumped into Professor Young!

"It's lucky you're here, professor," Joe blurted, and quickly described their pursuit of the bearded man with the tinted glasses.

"I saw him!" Young declared. "He got out of the elevator and went up to the next floor. You may be able to catch him!"

The boys rushed up, found no one on the second floor, and continued to the top. There was no sign of the man anywhere! Joe and Smoky asked a group of students if they had seen him. No one had.

"He must have gone down the back stairs," said a girl.

The boys returned to the ground floor. Young was still there and told them he had been watching the main staircase. "I was ready to call for help if the man appeared, but he didn't."

"He probably took the back staircase," Joe said.

"Too bad," Young said. "Well, I hope you catch him next time. I'll keep an eye open and have him arrested if he shows up at the lab again.

By the way, he apparently got in yesterday by flashing someone else's pass. An employee reported that his was stolen. But now that everyone's alerted, the fellow won't be able to pull the same trick twice."

Young walked off to work in the card-index file, and Smoky said he had to get going, too. He returned to the bookstack he had been examining before, while Joe went to question the attendant at the door.

"A man with tinted glasses and a beard?" the fellow said. "Yes, he walked out a few minutes ago."

"Thank you," Joe said. Disappointed, he joined Frank and Chet and told them about his unsuccessful pursuit.

"Don't worry. I'm sure we'll see our shadow again," Frank muttered. "Meanwhile we looked at all the books, including the one you pulled halfway off the shelf. We didn't find anything interesting on Woomera, so let's get over to the lab and start working."

The trio spent the rest of the week questioning employees and students at the lab, searching files and records, and investigating Dr. Jenson's background and family. Not a single clue turned up.

As they were painstakingly searching the scientist's desk, Frank noticed a lightning bolt engraved on one side. He asked Professor Young about it.

"That's Adrian's unofficial trademark," Young

told them. "The staff claims he solves problems with lightning speed, and one of the fellows
marked his desk one day after Adrian helped him
out on a critical project."

On Sunday night the phone rang as the boys
were getting ready for bed. Frank lifted the receiver. "It's Dad," he called out. Joe and Chet
joined him at the instrument and filled the elder
Hardy in on what they had done in Princeton.

"I'm still investigating people at the Space
Flight Center," Fenton Hardy said. "Director
Henry Mason is afraid that an attempt may be
made to destroy the rocket on its pad. I joined the
work crew in disguise and spent two days at the
launch site. However, so far I'm up against a stone
wall."

"Will you stay there until the launching?"
Frank asked.

"Yes, I think so. It will take a lot more leg work
to uncover a lead. Also, I'm setting up a brand-
new security system for the launching. It's of vital
importance that nothing go wrong."

"What do you suggest we do?" Frank asked.
"We've talked to everyone in the lab and nothing
has turned up."

His father was thoughtful for a moment, then
said, "I think your best bet is to go to Australia!"

CHAPTER VII

Radioactive Evidence

"AUSTRALIA!" Frank exclaimed.

"Yes. Tell Professor Young I want you to try to pick up Jenson's trail in Sydney. A room was booked for him at the Australian Arms Hotel, but apparently he never checked in."

"Okay, Dad. We'll go as soon as we can."

"And another thing. Try to shake your shadow. He worries me. He obviously knows you're investigating the case and follows you wherever you go."

"We'll get rid of him on the way home," Frank promised and hung up.

"Do you think Young will let me go along?" Chet asked apprehensively.

"We'll ask him," Frank said and called the professor's home. He told Young about the conversation with his father and the detective's suggestion.

"That's a good idea," Young agreed. "Your father is right. You're being watched here. So far I haven't been able to find out anything about your shadow, and it's probably best if you leave Princeton without returning to the lab. Take a roundabout route and make sure you're not being tailed."

"Will do," Frank said. "If I can't get plane reservations for tomorrow or Tuesday, I'll call you back. Can we take Chet with us?"

Young hesitated. "I'm responsible for the expenses in this case, Frank. I can't really make a requisition for three people without a pressing reason."

"I understand," Frank said, disappointed.

Chet, who had overheard the conversation, looked crestfallen. After Frank hung up, he patted his friend on the back. "Don't feel bad, Chet. We might be back sooner than you think."

"Feel bad!" Chet said. "I feel worse! I would love to see the kangaroos and the Great Barrier Reef. Just think of skin diving in the coral reef, more than a thousand miles of it! And fish in all colors of the rainbow——"

"Listen, we're not going sightseeing. We have a mystery to solve," Joe put in. "Now I'd better call the airline and make reservations."

Frank and Joe booked a flight to Sydney on Tuesday. Early Monday morning the boys left the Nassau Club and drove home, making sure they were not followed.

"The coast is clear," Joe reported. "No one is behind us."

They were not far out of Princeton, however, when Chet noticed a black limousine that seemed to keep them in sight. When Frank stepped on the gas, the driver of the limousine followed suit.

"You'll have to get off this road to lose him," Joe said to his brother. But before Frank had a chance to do this, the limousine pulled nearly abreast of them. The driver honked his horn and motioned for them to pull to the side.

"Make a run for it!" Joe advised and Frank pressed the accelerator to the floor.

Another car drove between the limousine and the Hardys. Their pursuer swerved to the left, increased the speed of his powerful V-8 engine, and passed the second vehicle. He inched up to the Hardys and proceeded to cut them off!

Frank noticed the legend on the limousine's side: PRINCETON AEROSPACE LABORATORY, as he wrenched the wheel desperately to avoid a crash. With split-second timing he turned to the right, past the front fender of the limousine, careened off the highway into a rest area, and skidded halfway around before coming to a stop in a cloud of dust.

The limousine jolted after him and its driver braked to a halt. He bent his head and seemed to be searching for something in the seat beside him. Neither Frank nor Joe got a good look at him, but they wasted no time. They leaped from their car and wrenched open the door of the limousine. In a split second they collared the man and wrestled him out.

"Hey, fellows, wait a minute!" the driver pleaded. *He was Smoky Rinaldo!*

Frank dropped Smoky's arm. "You nearly caused a crack-up!" he said angrily.

"Is this another one of your practical jokes?" Joe almost shouted.

"Of course not," Smoky said. "But I had to catch you, and you ignored the horn when I tried to flag you down. You wouldn't stop, so I had to make you!"

"We thought you were the guy who followed us all over Princeton," Joe said, his anger cooling.

"I assumed you'd recognize me."

"With that goofy cap pulled down over your face?"

"Anyway, I didn't mean to cause an accident," Smoky went on. "I thought I could detour you into the rest area by cutting you off."

"What did you want to stop us for?" asked Chet, who had joined the boys.

Smoky held up his hand and revealed a metal flask with Dr. Jenson's name on it. "Here, look at this!"

"What about it?" Frank asked.

"It's radioactive!" Smoky asserted.

Chet retreated hurriedly. "It might explode!"

"Radioactive material doesn't just explode," Frank calmed him. "It takes a triggering device to start a chain reaction."

Smoky swung his flask by its heavy top. "No fear of that. It's not even radioactive enough to kill a cockroach."

Frank was getting irritated. "Did you chase us all the way from Princeton to tell us that?"

"No. I wanted you to know that I think Dr. Jenson was up to something."

"Why?"

"Because I found this flask in one of the file cabinets. I was digging in some records and ran across the flask in the back of the bottom drawer. It's against regulations for anyone to take anything radioactive out of the lab."

Smoky explained that the steel flasks were used to hold nuclear materials during experiments. When the experiment ended, the scientist conducting it was supposed to send his flasks to a storeroom lined with lead, where they would be decontaminated.

"Dr. Jenson took this one and hid it in the file," Smoky concluded. "He shouldn't have done that."

"Did he ever break the rules before?" Joe asked.

"I have no idea."

"Did you tell Professor Young about it?"

"Sure. Right away."

"What did he say?"

"He found it very odd and called you at the

Nassau Club. He was informed that you had just left. Since he didn't know what arrangements you had made and whether you would go home before you left for Australia, he asked me to try to catch up with you. He also gave me a photo of Jenson for you. So I drove in the direction of Bayport. I figured I'd go down the highway for a while, and sure enough, I saw your car."

Frank was thoughtful. "This is odd. I'm glad you caught us, Smoky."

"One thing bothers me," Joe said. "We searched all the files in his office and the flask was not there then."

"It wasn't in his office. It was in the record room." Smoky said. "In one of the general files that a number of people use. But it was Jenson's flask, all right, none of the others have any occasion to handle radioactive materials." He looked at the three boys. "Now you're not mad any more that I cut you off?"

"Of course not. You had no choice," Frank told him.

"Okay. I'll head back then. And good luck to you. I hope you find Dr. Jenson!" Smoky got into the limousine and drove off.

Frank, Joe, and Chet resumed their trip to Bayport and discussed the latest development.

"How about that!" Chet said. "I wonder why Jenson hid that radioactive flask in the general file?"

"Maybe he was going to smuggle it out of the lab," Joe suggested, "to hand it over to someone on the outside. The more I think about it, the more I'm convinced that he wasn't kidnapped by foreign agents after all. He made a deal with them!"

Frank was doubtful. "What could anybody do with a radioactive flask?"

"I don't know. They might analyze the atomic formula from the stuff in the flask," Joe guessed.

"Okay," Frank gave in. "But where does that leave the warning message Smoky found under the blotter on Jenson's desk?"

"Jenson himself might have planted it there to throw people off his trail," Chet said.

"I don't know," Frank mused. "Suppose his kidnappers did it to mislead us after they grabbed him? And, frankly, I have my doubts about Smoky. He found the note and the bottle. Yet, Young assured us that Jenson's desk was searched. How do we know that Smoky didn't plant the stuff?"

"Aw, Frank," Chet said impulsively, "Smoky's a nice guy. He wouldn't do anything like that."

"Frank's right," Joe said. "We can't take anything for granted, not even that Smoky is a nice guy."

Chet sighed. "I don't know what to think any more. I give up."

"Let's call Dad before we leave and ask him to

check out Smoky," Joe said. "And we'll call Professor Young to make sure he sent Smoky after us."

Some time later the trio rolled into Bayport. The Hardys dropped Chet at the Morton farm on the outskirts of town, then continued to their house, where they were welcomed by their mother and aunt.

"I'm so glad you're back!" Mrs. Hardy said, giving them each a hug.

"Not for long," Frank told her.

"What do you mean?"

"We're leaving for Australia tomorrow!"

"Australia? Hmph, next thing you'll be taking off for Mars," Aunt Gertrude grumbled. "Now tell us what this is all about."

The boys did, and Gertrude Hardy frowned. "Do you suppose this missing scientist could have been captured by headhunters?"

"I doubt it," said Frank, keeping a straight face. "The Australian abos aren't headhunters, Aunty, and they don't run wild in Sydney."

"I know that," Miss Hardy snapped. "You didn't say he disappeared in Sydney."

"Well, that's where his trail ends, anyhow." Frank grinned and turned to his brother. "I'm going to call Professor Young."

"Good idea," Joe said. "I'll come with you."

They called Princeton, and the professor verified what Smoky had told them. "We didn't check that file because Dr. Jenson seldom used it," he said. "I'm sure it was his flask, though, because he wrote his name on it, and I know his handwriting. When are you leaving?"

"Tomorrow," Frank said. "We'll get in touch with you when we find a lead."

When Frank put the receiver back into the cradle, Joe said, "While you're at it, would you call Mr. Ponsley? We'll have to tell him that we can't work for him."

"Sure." Frank dialed the man's number. "This is Frank Hardy," he said a few seconds later. "I'm sorry we can't take the Moran assignment, but we're involved in our father's case and have to leave the country."

Ponsley was unhappy. "That is disappointing news. I was counting on you to locate Michael," he said. "Well, I'll have to get another detective. I need one now more than ever, because I have a new clue!"

CHAPTER VIII

Danger in the Surf

FRANK started to ask what the new clue was, but a loud click at the other end of the line told him that the man had hung up.

"Mr. Ponsley says he has a new lead on Mike Moran," Frank said to Joe.

"What is it?"

"Don't know. He didn't tell me. Anyhow, it doesn't matter. We're tied up with the Jenson investigation. Somebody else will have to find Mike, wherever he is."

Early next morning the boys packed their bags and were just about ready to depart for the airport, when Chet arrived in his jalopy.

"Guess what!" he called out, bubbling over with excitement.

"What?" Frank asked.

"I won first prize in my category of the science competition, fifteen hundred dollars in cash!"

"Wow, that's great, Chet!" Joe exclaimed. "Have you decided what to do with it yet?"

"Sure! I'll go to Australia with you guys, of course!" Chet said. "I already called the airline. They had a vacant seat on your plane, so I packed my bags and came over here pronto!"

"That's terrific!" Frank said. "I'm glad you can come with us."

"So am I," Joe added. "And now we'd better leave so we don't miss our flight."

The boys said good-by to Mrs. Hardy and Aunt Gertrude and drove to the Bayport airfield, where they parked their car in an overnight lot. They took a plane to New York and transferred at Kennedy Airport to a jumbo jet for Sydney, Australia.

Soon they had settled into their seats at the rear of the plane. Chet sat at the window, Frank in the middle, and Joe on the aisle. Frank took a map of the Pacific from a folder provided by the airline and began to plot their route.

"We'll touch down at Los Angeles and Honolulu," he informed his companions. "From there it's nonstop to Sydney."

The plane took off. Suddenly a flash of red caught Joe's eye. A stout man was napping on the other side of the aisle, a few rows in front of the boys. The color came from a large ruby ring he wore.

Joe stood up to see better. "That's Ponsley!" he exclaimed.

Frank picked up the map spread across his knees and got up, too. He looked where his brother was pointing. "It sure is, Joe. What's he doing here?"

"Maybe he's tailing us," Chet guessed.

"Well, if he is, he's not very good at it," Joe replied. "He's asleep, and that giant ruby is a dead giveaway. Let's wake him up."

"Not me," Chet said hastily. "I'll stay in this seat until we land!"

Leaving their friend, Frank and Joe walked up the aisle. Joe nudged their portly acquaintance with his elbow.

Ponsley stirred, yawned, opened his eyes, and stared at the Hardys. He looked startled as he recognized them.

"Are you following us?" Joe demanded.

"Of course not," Ponsley replied.

"How come you're on this plane, then?" Frank asked.

"Senator Moran had a tip from a friend who just returned from abroad," Ponsley explained. "The man said he recognized Michael in a newspaper photograph of a soccer game in Sydney. The senator didn't give me time to find another detective. He told me to go to Australia myself, so I caught this plane and here I am."

"Quite a coincidence," Frank commented.

"That's right," Ponsley challenged. "What are *you* doing on this plane?"

"I told you we had to leave the country," Frank pointed out. "Our investigation led us to Sydney."

Ponsley beamed and gestured with his hand, causing his ruby ring to throw off rays of deep red. "Wonderful!" he exclaimed. "Both investigations will take place in Sydney. You can work on them at the same time!"

The Hardys talked it over and concurred that they might handle the two cases while they were in Australia.

"That's okay," Frank told Ponsley, "but our assignment comes first. We can't let the search for Mike Moran get in the way of that."

"All right," Ponsley said. "I'm glad you'll help me. After all, I really am not a detective!"

The Hardys returned to their seats and informed Chet about their conversation with Ponsley. Then they settled back for the rest of the flight to Los Angeles, where some passengers got off, others got on, and the jet became airborne again. The boys napped as it crossed the California coastline and headed out over the Pacific. Finally the Hawaiian Islands came into view, and soon they landed in Honolulu.

The captain's voice came over the intercom. "Please disembark. There will be a delay because of a technical problem."

Everybody went down the steps and into the terminal, where a stewardess informed them that the delay would last overnight. "A bus is ready to take you all to a hotel on Waikiki Beach," she said. "We'll continue the flight in the morning."

The boys and Ponsley boarded the bus with the other passengers and an hour later they had checked in at a luxurious hotel. From their window, the three Bayporters could see the broad band of white sand where the waters of the Pacific lapped ashore. White foam formed where the breakers rolled in. Surfboard riders tried to keep their footing on huge swells that carried them forward at express-train speeds, and most fell into the water. The rest glided triumphantly to the beach.

"What say we try it, too?" Joe asked.

"Affirmative," Frank replied.

"I'll show you how to ride a surfboard!" Chet boasted. "Lead me to it!"

They called Ponsley and asked him if he wanted to join them.

"No thanks," he replied. "I'll take a walk instead."

Leaving him in the hotel, the boys went to the bathhouse, rented swim trunks, and toted surfboards into the water. They pushed through the shallow waves and reached the point far out where breakers began to form.

"Last one in gets the booby prize!" Chet shouted gleefully, as he climbed up and balanced himself with his arms stretched out. A breaker caught hold of his board and sent it flying toward the beach.

Frank and Joe followed on either side. The

three made long curves up and down over the ocean swells, and they leaned to one side or the other to compensate for the tilt of their boards. Sunlight gleamed off the water and the wind blew spray into their faces.

Chet had a lead at the start, but Frank and Joe skillfully maneuvered over the turbulent breakers until they were zooming along just behind him.

Then a wave cutting across the breakers at an angle struck Chet's surfboard, knocking it around. The heavy impact caused him to lose his footing and he tumbled into the water. His crazily floating board whacked him on the side of the head and he sank out of sight!

Frank dived from his own board into the water in Chet's direction, and Joe came headlong after him. They groped underwater as long as they could hold their breaths. Forced to surface, the Hardys gulped air and looked around frantically. Chet's head bobbed up near Joe. His eyes were closed, and his body limp. Presently he slipped below the surface again!

"He's out cold!" Frank yelled. "Grab him before he disappears!"

Joe did a seal flip that took him arching from the surface down into the depths, where he spotted Chet being dragged toward the open sea by a strong undertow. Using the breaststroke and kicking his feet hard, Joe reached his friend and pushed him to the surface. Frank splashed over, crooked an elbow under Chet's chin, and swam on his back in the direction of the shore. Joe, who surfaced beside them, gave Frank a hand with his burden. As they touched the sand in the shallow water, Chet came to. The three stumbled onto the beach and sat down, gasping for breath.

A lifeguard jogged across the sand. "That was a great rescue," he complimented the Hardys. "I didn't come in because I could see you had the situation under control." He turned to Chet. "How do you feel?"

Chet rubbed his head. "Okay, I guess," he mumbled. "But I sure have a powerful headache. I'm going back to the hotel. Besides, I'm nauseated from swallowing half the Pacific."

He got to his feet and walked off. Frank and Joe went with him. They insisted that he see the hotel doctor, whose prognosis was that Chet would be fit again after a night's sleep. The diagnosis was correct. Chet woke up in the morning with nothing more than tenderness on the side of his head.

After breakfast the bus took all the passengers back to the airport, and soon they were on their way again. They flew southwest across what seemed to be an endless expanse of ocean before Samoa came into view. The boys talked to Ponsley for a while, then went back to their seats to read.

They stopped when the stewardess served their meals. Chet ravenously dug into everything that was put in front of him, looking blissful.

"Chet, there's nothing like chow to bring you back to normal," Frank declared.

"Lucky the airline doesn't have to feed you every day," Joe needled him. "It would go broke."

Chet downed the last mouthful of cherry pie. "That'll hold me for a while," he predicted.

The stewardess removed the trays and the boys dozed off until the plane ran into turbulence and began to wobble.

Chet opened his eyes, slumped in his seat, and placed a hand on his belt buckle. "I don't feel so good," he confessed.

As the turbulence increased, the plane bounced up and down. Chet turned pale. His freckles stood out and his eyes bulged. "What's happening?" he muttered fearfully.

"We're in the jetstream, that's all," Frank reassured him. "We'll soon be out of it."

Suddenly the plane flew into a downdraft and dropped a number of feet.

"We're gonna crash!" Chet cried. Desperately he clawed the life jacket from under his seat, slipped it on, and pulled the strings, triggering the inflation mechanism. The life jacket ballooned out, pinning Chet between the seats.

A stewardess rushed up. "Sir, what are you doing?" she demanded.

Chet closed his eyes and gasped. "If we survive the crash, we'll all drown!"

CHAPTER IX

The Porter's Clue

"NONSENSE!" the stewardess retorted sternly. "We are not going to crash!"

Chet opened one eye. "We aren't?"

"Certainly not. Turbulence in the air is routine! You are disturbing the other passengers."

Frank hastily assured her that he and Joe would take care of the situation. The stewardess thanked him and moved toward the cockpit. By now the jet was flying steadily on course. Frank let the air out of the life jacket, helped Chet wriggle out of it, and stowed it under the seat.

Chet swallowed hard and looked remorseful. "I thought we'd crash for sure," he said.

"Forget it," Joe said. "No harm done."

"Get ready for Australia, Chet," Frank advised.

The freckle-faced youth regained his composure. His broad grin returned. "Kangaroos! Boomerangs! I can't wait!"

Finally they could see the coastline of Australia as the plane thundered down over Port Jackson, a large bay with long watery indentations into the land. Sydney Harbor came into view, spanned by a long suspension bridge.

"When we were reading up on Australia," Joe said, "I remember one of the books said the people in Sydney call that bridge 'the coathanger.'"

The boys could see big ocean-going ships tied up at the docks, and clusters of tall buildings. The city and its suburbs lay spread out below them in a pattern of streets, squares, and parks, illuminated by the evening sun.

The plane landed at the airport. After getting through customs, the boys and Ponsley took a taxi to their hotel. They had booked rooms at the Australian Arms, where Dr. Jenson had also made a reservation before he disappeared.

"May as well start our detective work right now," Frank decided.

As they got out of their taxi, he showed the hotel porter photos of Dr. Jenson and Mike Moran.

"Recognize these people?" Frank queried.

The porter studied the faces and shook his head. "I've never seen either of them," he declared.

They made the same inquiry at the hotel desk, but to no avail. During dinner, they discussed how they should proceed.

"We ought to check with police headquarters

first thing in the morning," Frank decided. "By now they may have some news on Dr. Jenson, and they may know something about Mike Moran, too."

"I'm going with you," Ponsley declared.

"Good. We'll meet for breakfast at eight," Frank said; then they retired for the night.

The following morning the Hardys got up bright and early. Chet did not feel well and decided to sleep a little longer.

"We'll see you when we come back," Joe told him, then he and Frank met Ponsley in the cafeteria. They had a quick breakfast and an hour later took a taxi to police headquarters. Here they explained their mission to a sergeant on duty.

"You'll have to talk to Inspector Morell," the sergeant replied. "He's in charge of the search for that missing Yank scientist. But he's not here right now. Should be back in half an hour."

"Okay, we'll talk to him later." Frank added that they were also trying to trace another missing American, named Michael Moran, whose face had been spotted in a Sydney newspaper photo.

"Hmm." The sergeant rubbed his jaw thoughtfully. "We don't keep tabs on all the tourists who come here—unless they get in trouble, of course. Let me just check with our Criminal Records Office."

He picked up the phone, dialed, and conversed for a few minutes. Then he hung up with a grin.

"You're in luck, mates. Our computer turned up his name straightaway. He's listed as a witness to an auto accident about a month ago. Gave his address as Flynn's Guesthouse on St. James Road."

The boys and Ponsley thanked the sergeant and took another cab to the guesthouse on St. James Road. They were disappointed, however, when the owner informed them that Mike Moran had departed about three weeks before, saying only that he was leaving town.

"So Moran's trail ends right here," Joe said glumly.

"And we haven't even picked up Jenson's yet," Frank added.

"What'll we do now, go around with the photographs?" Ponsley asked.

"Right. Let's start here," Joe said. He showed the owner Jenson's picture, but the man told them he had never seen the American before. Then the group walked out into the street. The boys returned to police headquarters while Ponsley took a taxi to their hotel.

After the Hardys had introduced themselves to Inspector Morell, he said, "I was just about to call Professor Young at the Aerospace Lab. We have traced Dr. Jenson to a shabby place on Sixteen Wallaby Drive. There was a fire there recently in the lobby that destroyed the hotel register and forced the owner to close for a while. That's why it took so long to track Jenson down."

The boys noted the address and thanked Inspector Morell. Then they took a taxi to Wallaby Drive. It was in a rundown section of town and number 16 looked like a decrepit apartment building. Only a small faded sign over the door indicated that it was a hotel. The blackened woodwork around the doors and windows showed signs of a recent blaze.

"I wonder if that fire the inspector mentioned was an arson job," Frank mused.

"That's an idea," Joe said. "Maybe someone was trying to keep the police from finding out Jenson stayed there."

The boys went inside. Two men stood behind the desk in the empty hallway that now served as a lobby. One was the manager, the other had "porter" stitched on the breast pocket of his threadbare jacket.

When Frank inquired about Jenson, the manager looked annoyed. "I've already told the police all I know," he said curtly. "Dr. Jenson left with two Americans the day after he checked in and I never heard from him again."

"Did he pay his bill?" Joe inquired.

"The men did."

"Why not Dr. Jenson himself?"

"How do I know?" the manager asked gruffly.

There was a brief silence before Frank said, "Were you afraid of trouble if you told the police too much about Jenson?"

The man's face turned sullen. "Whatever gave you that idea?"

"You had a fire here, for one thing. And maybe you received some threats."

"I dunno what you're talking about."

Frank flashed a twenty dollar bill. "Try to remember. Was there anything even the slightest bit unusual about Jenson's departure?"

The manager hesitated, obviously tempted. He glanced furtively around, then took the money and quickly put it in his wallet. "Well, Jenson seemed drunk," he told the boys. "He was sort of slumped between these two blokes. They paid and led him outside, then pushed him into a car and drove off."

"Do you think he was forced to go with them?"

"I dunno. I think he was drunk."

"Can we look in his room for a clue?" Joe asked. "We must find him!"

"Go ahead. I haven't rented it since." The manager gave him the key and the boys went into Jenson's room.

Joe looked into the closet while Frank went through the bureau drawers. They turned the wastebasket upside down, and lifted the mattress from the bed.

"Nothing here," said Joe, standing in the middle of the room and gazing around. His eyes fell on the door, which was covered with scratches and graffiti. Joe went over and bent down, staring at the bottom panel.

"Hey Frank, come here a minute!"

Frank looked at the initials and sentences

scribbled on the lower part of the door. "Graffiti," he said. "Courtesy of the hotel's high-class clientele."

"Look close," Joe advised. "See this sign?"

"A bolt of lightning!" Frank exclaimed. "The same as we saw on Dr. Jenson's desk!"

"Correct. And after it are the letters Al S. What do you think that means?"

"Maybe those are the initials of Dr. Jenson's kidnapper!" Frank said, excited. "Could be his name is Albert Smith."

"Or Alfred Scott, or a million other combinations," Joe commented.

Their enthusiasm diminished as they realized the number of possibilities. "There are too many names with those initials," Frank concluded. "We'll have to find Jenson to find out whom he meant."

"Let's think about it as we go back to our hotel," Joe suggested. "What say we walk instead of taking a cab?"

"Suits me," Frank agreed.

Before leaving, they wrote down their room number at the Australian Arms and asked the manager to call them if he remembered any other details. Then they walked toward the center of the city, which was not far, and found that Sydney was built on a number of hills. Rows of houses painted in bright colors lined the streets, and cars whizzed back and forth through narrow thoroughfares.

"Why do you think Jenson checked into that crummy hotel?" Joe asked his brother.

"Maybe he suspected he was being followed and wanted to hide," Frank replied.

"Or, if he's not on the level, perhaps he wanted to disappear and obscure his tracks," Joe concluded.

"I think he was kidnapped. I don't believe he was drunk when those guys took him out of the place," Frank said.

"You're probably right. Boy, these streets are all uphill or downhill," Joe said. "I'm getting tired!"

"Cheer up. We're coming close to level ground," Frank told him. He referred to Macquarie Street, where they saw the law courts before cutting over to George Street, the site of the magnificent Town Hall and St. Andrew's Cathedral.

They stepped off the curb and began to cross over to the cathedral, when a car swished around the corner and barreled straight at them at top speed!

Instinctively Frank and Joe whirled to leap back onto the sidewalk. The car followed them, heading them off. Again they raced into the street, hoping to make it to the other side. The car careened after them. It was a wild chase until Frank slipped and fell. The car hurtled straight at him!

Joe barely had time to shove his brother out of

the way. There was no chance to escape himself. He took a death-defying leap at the car, sprawling across the hood to avoid being run down!

The car zoomed past Frank, missing him by inches, and jolted over a patch of grass bordering the sidewalk. Joe was blocking the driver's view, but a sharp twist of the wheel sent the youth sliding off. He rolled over and over. Only the cushion of grass saved him from serious injury.

As Joe lay half-stunned, he caught a parting glimpse of the bearded driver, scowling at him through the open window as the car roared away. The man was wearing tinted glasses!

He continued up the street, rounded the corner, and vanished. Frank and Joe got to their feet, shaking their heads at their narrow escape. The few pedestrians ran to help, but nobody had caught the car's license number.

"Thanks for saving me, Joe," Frank puffed. "Are you okay?"

"Yeah, except that fall rattled my eyeteeth." The younger Hardy waited till they were alone again before adding, "Did you get a look at the driver?"

"No. Who was he?"

"The guy who shadowed us in Princeton!"

Frank gave a long whistle. "He followed us to Australia! How did he know we'd be here?"

"He didn't follow us to Bayport," Joe said. "And I watched on the way to the airport. No one was behind us."

Joe took a death-defying leap at the car.

"Maybe he overheard our telephone conversation with Professor Young," Frank said. "Or he could have overheard Young and Smoky talking when the professor told Smoky to catch us before we left for Australia."

"Or Smoky could have told him!" Joe added.

"Right. Once he knew we were coming here, all he had to do was check with the airlines and take an earlier flight or even get on the same plane with us in disguise!"

"This is getting serious," Joe said. "The guy's out to kill us. If we don't crack this case soon, he may succeed!"

Taking various detours, the boys returned to the Australian Arms Hotel. When they arrived in their room, Chet was still sleeping. Frank woke him up and told him what had happened. He was just about finished when the telephone rang. Joe picked it up.

He heard a muffled voice say, "If you want information on Dr. Jenson, be at the Botany Bay Coffeehouse in King's Cross in one hour!"

CHAPTER X

A Spy in the Crowd

"WHO are you and how will we know you?" Joe asked.

"I'll know you, and that's all that matters." The phone went dead. Joe relayed the message to Frank and Chet.

"Sounds like a trap," he added. "Probably another one of our shadow's tricks."

"I think we should chance it," Frank said. "We don't have any other leads in the case."

There was a knock on the door. Frank walked over to it and asked, "Who is it?"

"Ponsley." It was their friend's familiar voice. Frank let him in and brought him up-to-date on the latest news.

"Suppose," Ponsley said, "I go along and trail behind you. If the crooks gang up on you, I'll call for help."

"Great idea!" Joe said. "How about you, Chet?"

Chet was awake by now, and felt better. "Of course, I'm coming, too," he said.

"Wait a minute," Frank objected. "I think it will be better if we split forces. You stay here, Chet, and if we're not back in an hour, alert the police. If you come along, they might get all of us and no one would know we're missing."

"Okay," Chet agreed readily. The thought of being caught did not appeal to him at all. Ponsley looked a bit doubtful, too, but did not retract his offer.

The three left, and just before the hour was up, the Hardys entered the Botany Bay Coffeehouse, a popular gathering place for Australians of all types from Sydney businessmen to shop girls, office workers, and people in the arts. Like most Aussies, they seemed to have a sun-tanned breezy look about them that the boys liked. Over coffee and tea, a babble of cheerful voices could be heard.

Frank and Joe sat down at a table in a corner and ordered coffee. They surveyed the room without spotting a familiar face until Ponsley walked in. He took a table on the opposite side of the room, winked to indicate that he was keeping them under surveillance, and told a waitress to bring him a pot of tea.

"You're right on time," a voice said at Frank's elbow. "You must be interested."

It was the porter from the hotel Dr. Jenson had stayed in!

The man sat down and accepted a cup of coffee. "Look, mates," he said in a low tone, "I know about Dr. Jenson. I opened the door for him and the two blokes who were with him. I could tell from the look in his eyes that he was drugged. When they pushed him into the car, he began to struggle. I went out to see what was going on, and I heard him mutter something."

"What was it?" Frank asked eagerly.

"He said 'Alice Springs' just before they slammed the door and drove off!"

"Why didn't you mention this before?" Joe inquired.

"I told the manager. He said he didn't want any trouble, and that I might have made a mistake. That's why I couldn't tell you at the hotel that I recognized Jenson's photo. After thinking it over, I thought you should know that he wasn't drunk. He was drugged!"

The porter drained his coffee cup and, after accepting some money from Frank in payment for his information, he rose to his feet. He was due back at the hotel and strode off. The Hardys stared at each other in consternation.

Joe broke the silence. "Now we know what Al S stands for. Alice Springs! She must be the leader of the kidnap gang. Maybe she's holding Jenson a prisoner right now here in Sydney!"

"Joe, Alice Springs isn't a person. It's a place— a town way off in the Outback in the middle of the country. Jenson left a message saying that he was taken to Alice Springs!" Frank said.

Joe jumped up from his chair. "This is a hot clue, Frank! We'll have to go to Alice Springs!"

"That's the way I see it. We'd better get out there in a hurry."

Ponsley left his table and joined them. "Who was that fellow and what did he say?"

Frank told him and repeated the conversation.

"Where is Alice Springs?" Ponsley asked.

"Let's find out," Frank suggested and pulled a map of Sydney from his pocket that showed all of Australia on the reverse side. He spread it flat on the table, running a fingertip from Sydney west across New South Wales into South Australia, and then up into the Northern Territory. His finger stopped almost exactly in the center of the continent, where the words "Alice Springs" were printed in black letters.

They could tell from the relief coloring that the town nestled in the foothills of the Macdonnell Ranges, at a point where a number of streams converged. The illustrations indicated that all around Alice Springs there were homesteads, mines, and cattle ranches.

Ponsley was aghast. "Impossible!" he cried, thumping the table with his fist until the ruby on his finger seemed to be a streak of red in the air. "That town is over a thousand miles from here!"

"A long trip," Joe agreed.

"Too long!" Ponsley snapped. "You have to stay in Sydney and continue the search for Mike Moran!"

Frank shook his head. "Mike will have to wait," he said firmly. "Jenson comes first. Besides, Mike said he was leaving town. Chances are he's not in Sydney anyway."

Ponsley groused and grumbled, but finally gave in. "I'll go with you," he decided. "I'm not the detective around here. I need you boys to solve my mystery. I'd better stay with you so I can be sure you start looking for Mike the minute you find Jenson."

"Fair enough," Frank said and paid the bill. He asked the waitress about the nearest travel bureau, which happened to be around the corner.

The boys were unable to book a scheduled flight for the next day, but the clerk referred them to the pilot of a small private plane, who had just come in to pick up possible fares.

"I belong to the Royal Flying Doctor Service," the pilot told them. "The RFDS flies doctors, nurses, and medicine over the Outback wherever someone is ill or injured. Planes are the only way to get around quickly in that area."

"You must be like the bush pilots in Alaska," Joe surmised. "They cover a lot of territory."

"Quite similar," the pilot agreed. "Well, I operate out of Alice Springs and will be flying back there tomorrow morning. I'll be glad to take you."

"We'll need four seats," Frank said. "A friend of ours is coming, too."

"That's okay. I have enough room."

The boys thanked the man and left the travel agency. "What say we call Chet to tell him the latest news, and then see a few more of the sights on the way back to the hotel?" Frank suggested.

"Good idea," Joe and Ponsley agreed. They called from a public phone booth, then strolled along the Elizabeth Street shopping area, glancing at items in store windows and enjoying the bustle of the city. They paused at a fishmonger's barrow.

"Anything on the menu from the Great Barrier Reef?" Frank inquired.

"Too far away, mate," the man laughed. "My fish come from Ulladulla, down south of here. How about some tasty snapper or John Dory? Blimey, you'll find 'em delicious!"

"Okay, you've convinced us." Joe chuckled.

They all bought fish sandwiches and munched them hungrily. Then they deposited their paper napkins in a trash bin and walked on.

Suddenly Frank spotted someone watching them from the opposite side of the street. The older Hardy boy recognized the man with the beard and the tinted glasses!

"Our shadow from Princeton!" he told his companions.

"The guy who tried to run us down!" Joe exploded. "Let's get him!"

The boys turned and hastened to the corner to cross Elizabeth Street. Ponsley brought up the rear as fast as he could. But the light turned red just as they arrived at the intersection and the flow of traffic compelled them to wait. By the time they got across, they could barely glimpse their quarry almost a block away.

"He's heading toward the waterfront!" Frank cried.

The Hardys and Ponsley ran after him. A sign, HARBOUR BRIDGE, pointed the way to the busy eight-lane steel span connecting Sydney to the North Shore.

Presently they came to the dock area, where ocean liners and tramp freighters were tied up at the piers to disgorge and take on passengers and cargo. Across the waters of Sydney Cove on their right could be seen the dazzling new opera house, looking like a cluster of pointed white concrete sails.

As the boys slowed to get their bearings, they almost bumped into a sailor who was hurrying in the opposite direction.

"Sorry, mates! I didn't see you coming," he apologized.

"Did you happen to pass a bearded man with dark glasses?" Frank asked him.

The sailor shoved back his cap and scratched

his head. "Don't recall noticing anyone like that," he replied, "but if you want to come back to me ship for a minute, I'll find out if anyone saw him."

"That's mighty kind of you, but weren't you going the other way? We don't want to hold you up."

"That's all right, cobber. I was just going on shore leave. Nothing that urgent."

Ponsley sat down on a wooden bollard to catch his breath. "I need a breather after all that running," he said. "You two go on. I'll wait here."

The boys accompanied the sailor to his freighter, which was moored nearby. On its stern was the name *Sydney Cove*.

The sailor grinned. "Recognize that name?"

Frank and Joe shook their heads. "Should we?" the younger Hardy boy asked.

"Maybe not, seeing as 'ow you're Yanks. But there once was a ship called *Sydney Cove* that sank. Only three 'ands survived to tell the tale. So now some say every ship with that name is jinxed."

Frank laughed. "We don't believe in jinxes."

The sailor grinned. "Then you got nothin' to fear. Come on aboard. You can call me Salty, by the way. Everyone else does."

He led the way up the gangplank to the well deck, where the captain was giving orders to his bosun and deck hands. One of the men was attaching a huge bale to a cargo boom near the open hold.

"What're you doing back aboard, Salty?" the officer bellowed.

"Just 'elpin' out these two Yanks, sir. They're lookin' for a bearded man with dark glasses. Anyone see 'im go by?"

The skipper and crewmen, who had stopped work, shook their heads. The boys thanked them and left the ship. They saw Ponsley coming toward them across the dock.

"I've seen enough of Sydney," he declared. "I'm going back to the hotel. Want to share a taxi with me?"

"May as well," Frank answered. "Looks like we've lost that creep we were chasing."

As they turned to go, the freighter's cargo boom swung out over the side with a heavy bale in its cargo net. The net opened just above the three and the bale hurtled down on them!

CHAPTER XI

Chet's Clever Plan

FRANK caught a glimpse of the bale as it tumbled out of the cargo net. "Watch out!" he shouted.

Frank and Joe lunged into Ponsley, pushing him out of the way and knocking him over backwards. The three went down in a tangle of arms and legs as the heavy cargo slammed into the dock a few feet away from them!

The Hardys got up but Ponsley lay still. Joe leaned over and shook him by the shoulders. "Mr. Ponsley, are you all right?" he asked, worried.

Ponsley groaned and stirred feebly.

"He's stunned," Frank judged. "He'll come around in a minute."

Salty hurried down the ship's gangplank to join them. "Blimey, I'm sorry!" he panted. "Someone swung the ruddy boom too far out. The net's not supposed to open till the operator presses the button. I don't know what 'appened. That bale might've 'urt you somethin' terrible!"

"It would have squashed us like beetles," Frank said. "But we're okay."

Ponsley sat up and opened his eyes. "Speak for yourself!" he cried. "I can hardly see! Good heavens, I think I'm going blind!"

Joe noticed that Ponsley's spectacles had been knocked off when he fell. The younger Hardy picked up the gold pince-nez, made sure the lenses had not been broken, and placed them back on Ponsley's nose.

"How's that?" he asked.

Ponsley adjusted the glasses with his thumb and forefinger. "Why, I can see again!" he said, relieved.

"We're not hurt, Salty," Frank told the sailor. "But I don't want to be in the way the next time your cargo net goes haywire."

Salty nodded and went back to the ship. Since Ponsley was more determined than ever to return to the hotel, they took a taxi to the Australian Arms.

When they stepped into the Hardys' room, they found it empty!

"Where's Chet?" Joe wondered.

"We'd better find out—fast," Frank replied tensely as he called the hotel desk. The clerk denied any knowledge of Chet's whereabouts. "Perhaps he went out for a newspaper," the man suggested.

The Hardys and Ponsley waited for an hour to see if Chet would come back, but there was no sign of him. Finally Frank jumped to his feet. "Joe, what if Chet has been kidnapped?"

"A dreadful thought!" Ponsley interjected.

As they considered what to do next, a key scraped in the lock. Somebody was trying to get in without being heard!

"It may be Chet's kidnapper!" Frank whispered.

The Hardys tiptoed across the room and stationed themselves on each side of the door, waiting for it to open.

The knob turned and the door swung inward. The mysterious visitor stealthily entered the room.

"Chet!" Frank and Joe cried in unison.

Their rotund friend closed the door quietly. Placing a finger on his lips, he jerked his head in the direction of the window, and led them over to it. He motioned them to stand back so as not to be seen and pointed to a department store across the street.

Two men were standing in front of it, watching the hotel. Another joined them and pointed at the boys' window. He had a black beard and wore tinted glasses! When a policeman came along, the men pretended to look at the display of clothes behind the glass panels. When he had passed, they resumed their vigil.

Chet tugged Frank's sleeve and drew his friends away from the window. "I noticed them right after you left," he reported.

"Obviously they stayed here while Tinted Glasses shadowed us through Sydney," Joe said.

"Maybe we should call the police," Chet suggested.

Frank shook his head. "They can't arrest these guys just because they're standing down there watching us. Besides, Tinted-Glasses and his partners might not know where Jenson is. Their only job may be to keep us from finding him. If we get tied up in a hassle between these guys and the law, that may be just what they want. It'll keep us from looking for Jenson."

Turning to Chet, Frank explained the clue they had just received, which pointed to Alice Springs as the next focus of their search.

"Gosh, stop to think of it," Chet said, "those lookouts may even be trying to find Jenson themselves—by shadowing *us*!"

"That's possible." Frank agreed. "Either way, I think our best bet is to give 'em the slip."

"How?" asked Joe.

His brother turned back to their chubby pal. "Does the hotel have a rear door?"

"I checked that," Chet replied. "Two more guys are out there in the alley. They look like they're ready to jump us if we leave."

"The roof!" Joe said. "Maybe we can try that."

Chet shook his head. "I went up there. There's a lookout on the opposite building. He's watching the fire escape. And there's no other exit."

"Then we're trapped!" Ponsley exclaimed.

"We are," Chet agreed. "But I've worked out an escape route!"

"How?" Frank asked.

"Just grab an overnight bag with a change of clothes and come with me," Chet said mysteriously. "Hurry up!"

Ponsley went to his room and was back shortly. The boys had each packed a small bag and were ready. Chet motioned them out of the room and locked the door carefully. Then he led the way to the freight elevator. They took it down to the basement, and followed Chet to a storeroom.

A tradesman was lifting empty crates into a truck backed up to the exit.

"These are the friends I told you about," Chet addressed him. "Since we left our belongings in our room, you know we're not trying to gyp the hotel. We're coming back."

"Righto," the man replied. "You paid me. Now I'll carry out my part of the bargain. Get into the truck, all of you, and lie low."

Chet climbed into the vehicle and edged his way toward the cab. Ponsley came next, then Frank and Joe. They crouched down behind the load of empty crates and the driver slammed the tailgate up. Then he went around to the cab, started the engine, and slowly moved the truck away from the hotel.

Through a crack in the tailgate Frank could see the two men in the alley watching the back door of the hotel.

"We outsmarted them after all!" he said with a chuckle. "They'll be standing there forever!"

The driver took them to George Street, where he stopped and let them off. "This is as far as you go," he said. "Good-by and good luck!"

The boys jumped out and thanked the man, then the truck sped away.

"I saw the truck coming up to the back door when I was in the basement," Chet revealed. "I figured the driver might make a deal with me, and he did."

"Good thinking, Chet," Joe complimented him.

Chet looked pleased. "What next?" he asked.

After a council of war, they decided to go to the airport and spend the night at a motel. From there, they phoned Inspector Morell and asked him to have the bearded man and his cohorts picked up for questioning. But an hour later Morell called back to report failure. Apparently the crooks had discovered that the Hardy boys and their friends had gotten away, and had abandoned their stakeout of the hotel.

Early next morning, the Hardys, Chet, and Ponsley took off for Alice Springs. The green areas around Sydney disappeared, and they found themselves flying deep into the Outback, where sand and huge stones extended to the horizon on all sides. Clusters of rocks ballooned from the desert floor into fantastic shapes.

"If we were in the States," Frank said, "I'd guess we were over Death Valley."

"Or the Dakota Badlands," Joe added.

"Well, it's hot and dusty here, too," the pilot pointed out. "There aren't any rattlesnakes down below, but there are Australian brown snakes, which are nearly as deadly."

"You are not going to land, are you?" Ponsley asked, frightened.

The pilot laughed. "Don't worry. Landing in this part of the Outback is the last thing I want to do."

The plane crossed rivers where good farmland spread along the banks. Big cattle ranches occupied hundreds of square miles beyond the Macdonnell Ranges in Australia's Northern Territory. Finally they landed at Alice Springs, and the four Americans got out. They stretched their muscles, cramped after the long flight, paid the pilot, and took a bus into town.

They found Alice Springs crisscrossed by rows of hardy trees that managed to stay alive in the arid soil. The buildings were mostly small and roofed with tin. On Anzac Hill, a shining monument commemorated the Australians and New Zealanders who fell in two world wars.

The boys stopped at police headquarters and asked about Jenson and Mike Moran. The officer on duty could supply no information on either, but gave the boys a list of hotels and guest houses where they could inquire.

"Good thing this town isn't big," Frank said.

"We won't have too much trouble checking these out."

"Are they all within walking distance?" Chet asked.

Frank had obtained a map of Alice Springs at the airport and looked at it. "I don't know. Let's start here and work toward the periphery of the town."

Checking with various hotels on the way, the four walked through Gorey's Arcade, the shopping center of Alice Springs. They went along the streets past bars and hamburger joints, and noticed that many men wore cowboy hats, shirts, trousers, and boots. Some of the men were dark-skinned "abos."

"Those guys look like they came from Tombstone with Wyatt Earp after the gunfight at the O.K. Corral!" Chet commented.

"Except that none of them carry six-shooters," Frank added with a grin.

They came to a fenced-in enclosure where a competition was being held. Cowboys lined the rails, waiting for their turn to rope steer and ride bucking broncos. Three judges on a raised platform judged the performances and awarded prizes.

"A rodeo!" Joe exclaimed. "How about that!"

"Let's spread out and keep our eyes open," Frank suggested. "There's always an outside chance of spotting Mike or Dr. Jenson in the crowd. While we're at it, we can chat with people, too, and find out if anybody has noticed an American answering either description. We'll meet here in half an hour."

"Good idea," Joe said, and the four separated and began buttonholing cowboys and spectators for information on the two missing men. None of the Australians had heard of them.

They were on the way to their meeting place again when the main event of the rodeo began. A rider came out of a chute, like a streak of lightning, on a coal-black horse that leaped and twisted in a savage effort to throw the man off its back.

Chet was fascinated by the violence of horse and rider contending to see who would win.

"I could get a better view from that fence post over there," he thought and climbed up. Carefully he positioned himself on the small post. But he got so involved in the show that at one point he lost his balance and dropped into the enclosure.

Frank, who saw the incident from a short distance away, muttered something about Chet and his ideas. Then the bronco threw its rider and charged full-tilt at Chet, who had just gotten to his feet.

"Watch out!" Frank yelled.

CHAPTER XII

Kangaroo Confrontation

CHET froze as the black horse, glaring and snorting, galloped toward him with pounding hooves!

Frank moved like lightning. He snatched a lasso that had been used in the steer-roping competition and hurled the noose in a long flying arc.

As it settled over the horse's neck, he fastened the other end of the lariat to a fence post. The enraged animal was about to trample Chet when the rope tightened and brought it to a rearing halt in a cloud of dust!

Chet scrambled over the fence and fought for breath. "Frank," he puffed, "you're better than those TV cowboys any day!"

There were loud cheers and a round of applause for Frank's rescue. One of the contestants came up and spoke to him admiringly. "Good-oh, cobber! Your China would've ended up a proper mess if you hadn't come through with that rope trick!"

"China?" Frank looked puzzled. "Is that a word you cowboys use down under?"

The Aussie laughed. "It's good old cockney rhyming slang—'China plate' for 'mate.' And we're not cowboys down here, Yank. We're stockmen. My name's John Harris."

Shaking hands, Frank introduced himself and his companions. Together they watched the rest of the rodeo, and Harris captured first prize for broncobusting. He invited them to join in the horseback ride around the ring. Ponsley quickly refused, saying he would rather wait on the viewing stand. He climbed up the few steps and sat down in a chair vacated by one of the rodeo judges.

Harris brought up three mounts. Frank, Joe, and Chet climbed into the saddles and trotted in the procession around the enclosure. The Hardys, who had ridden horseback many times, guided their mounts with practiced skill.

Chet clutched the reins with one hand, waved the other, and shouted, "This is for me!" His horse, feeling the tug of the bridle, thought it was time to rear up on its hind legs. The movement alarmed Chet, who slackened his grip and let the horse have its head.

Finally the ride ended, the rodeo broke up, and the boys joined Ponsley for a walk back toward the center. They checked two more hotels without luck, then stopped at a luncheonette and ordered hamburgers.

Chet pitched into his enthusiastically. "Nothing like a horseback ride to set you up for chow."

Frank laughed. "Chet, who was in charge, you or the horse?"

"Maybe you'd like an encore," Joe needled him. "We can go back if you like."

"No, thanks," Chet said. "I showed the rodeo what I can do. That's enough for me."

Ponsley was becoming annoyed. "This trip has not been a success," he argued. "I'm sure Dr. Jenson isn't here, and neither is Mike Moran."

Frank munched a pickle. "We only have a few more places to check, and we never give up prematurely."

Just then John Harris walked into the luncheonette, recognized the Americans, and came to their table.

"Mind if I join you?" he asked.

"Of course not," Frank said, inviting him to sit down. Harris ordered a hamburger. While he ate, Frank told him they were looking for two missing Americans. "Got any suggestions?"

Harris looked thoughtful. "I overheard a Yank talking to someone right here in this luncheonette not too long ago. He mentioned Cutler Ranch, a cattle station up north, owned by Americans."

Frank showed him the photographs. "Was it either of these two men?"

Harris shrugged. "He had his back turned to me. I just remember the accent, since it's rare in these parts."

Frank exchanged glances with his brother.

"Worth a try," Joe agreed.

"It's a long ride up north, beyond McGrath Creek and the Sandover River." Harris warned. "So pick a car that gets a lot of miles to the gallon. You won't pass any petrol pumps on the way."

Finishing his hamburger, he said good-by and left. Joe seemed to be watching someone. Presently he got up and muttered, "Let's go!"

Frank and the others paid their bill and followed Joe outside. But they had gone scarcely a block when Joe suddenly whirled around. His three companions saw him grab a seedy stranger in a battered, greasy-looking felt hat, who had been walking several paces behind them.

"Why are you following us, mister?" the younger Hardy demanded angrily.

The stranger cringed when he saw the fighting look on Joe's face. "You've got me all wrong, mate," he mumbled. "I wasn't following nobody."

"Don't give me that! You were eavesdropping on everything we said back there in the restaurant."

"Well. . . ." The stranger hesitated nervously, then blurted, "I expect I did listen closer'n I should've done. But I was worried about what that stockman was telling you. Didn't know if I ought to warn you or not."

Joe frowned. "Warn us about what?"

"The Cutlers."

"What about them?" Frank demanded.

"They're strange blokes. From what I hear, they don't welcome visitors—especially visitors who ask questions."

"How come?" Joe pressed.

The seedy stranger shrugged. "All I know is what I've heard some of the abos hereabouts say."

"What do they say?"

"That they've seen nosy swagmen ride up to the Cutlers' cattle station, but they've never seen none of them ride away again!"

The four Americans stared at the seedy stranger uneasily. Before they could cross-examine him, he wriggled free of Joe's grasp and hurried off down the street.

"What did he mean by 'swagmen'?" Chet asked with a worried, wide-eyed look.

"Traveling cowhands, carrying their 'swag' or personal belongings in a blanket roll," Frank explained. "I remember that much from what I read about the Outback."

"They may be traveling cowhands," said Ponsley, "but if what we just heard means anything, once they go nosing around the Cutlers' place, their travels come to a sudden end!"

Chet felt cold chills. "You really think the Cutlers polish off trespassers?"

"Suppose that guy was just trying to scare us off?" Joe suggested. "Suppose he doesn't want us to see something out there? Maybe Jenson is a prisoner at the Cutler Ranch and they don't want us to rescue him?"

Frank stood up. "It's still daylight. Let's go!"

Ponsley was against it. "I believe this will be another wild-goose chase," he protested.

"Mr. Ponsley, we can't stop now," Frank urged. "We know Americans took Jenson to Alice Springs. The Cutlers are Americans, and someone's trying to keep us away from their place. We have to see what's going on at the Cutler Ranch!"

"You can stay here until we get back," Joe proposed.

"No, no!" Ponsley objected. "I don't want to stay alone. I'll go with you!"

The group went to the only car-rental agency in town and selected a compact that gave them good mileage to the gallon.

"You're lucky," the agent told them. "We were all out of cars, but someone returned this one sooner than expected."

"Good," Frank said and paid for the rental. Then they drove north from Alice Springs with Joe at the wheel. The fertile region gave way to desert, after which signs of agriculture reappeared around McGrath Creek. They could see farmhouses with tall windmills pumping water from underground.

Soon the desert began again, and they were traveling a dusty road through desolate country marked by the bleached skeletons of horses and cows that had succumbed in the waterless waste.

"I believe we should pause for a rest," Ponsley finally said. "Let's stop here."

Joe pulled over to the side of the road, where a strange formation of huge rocks rose above the desert. They noticed that one of the rocks was covered with painted figures. A serpent wound its way in long sinuous coils up from the base of the cliff. On the left, an owl perched in a flutter of feathers, as if terrified by the snake. On the right, a kangaroo hopped fearfully out of the way. Above these animals, a medicine man wielded a magic wand to ward off the serpent's poison.

Chet scratched his head. "How did this guy and his pets get here?"

"The Aborigines painted them," Frank replied. "I read about their rock paintings when we were in Princeton. These could be hundreds of years old."

Ponsley nodded. "Terrific technique," he declared. "Compares favorably with modern art."

The four marveled at the figures done in white, black, brown, and dark red. At last, the boys sat down with their backs against the cliff. Ponsley, who complained about his stiff back, wandered away into the desert. A moment later he shouted frantically.

The boys scrambled to their feet and raced toward him, but stopped halfway, jarred by what they saw.

Their portly friend was confronted by a large kangaroo!

The animal stood on its hind legs with its heavy tail extended on the sand. Its fur was gray, shading to white underneath, and the tip of the tail was black. It held its small front paws up in the air and stared at Ponsley, who raised his hand in a frantic effort to frighten it off. His ruby ring glittered in the sun.

Suddenly the kangaroo began to hop toward him! The more Ponsley waved, the faster it bounded forward, its eyes fixed on his hand.

Frank recalled that kangaroos are attracted by bright objects. Obviously this one was after Ponsley's ruby ring!

"Stop waving!" the boy yelled, but Ponsley did not seem to hear him. He backed away from the kangaroo, turned frantically, and ran as fast as he could. The kangaroo also increased its speed, caught up with, and sprang at him in a high bound!

Ponsley's feet became entangled with one another, and he fell headlong into the sand. The kangaroo leaped clear over him! The boys yelled at the top of their lungs to frighten the creature, and, after landing on its strong hind legs, it hopped rapidly away into the distance.

The Hardys helped Ponsley up and brushed the sand off his suit. He was indignant about the kangaroo confrontation, and for the rest of the drive he kept insisting that they should never have ventured into the Outback.

They crossed the Sandover River and continued north until Frank spotted a large warning sign: CUTLER RANCH—KEEP OUT!

"Maybe we shouldn't drive in there," Chet advised.

"Hey, we've come all the way from Alice Springs to check this place out," Joe reminded him. "Besides, it's almost dark already and no one will see us." He switched off the headlights and turned up a rutted drive leading to the property. He drove slowly till they reached a wire fence with a gate. Beyond it stood the ranch house.

Joe stopped the car and the boys strained to look at the building. Suddenly a light snapped on in one window.

"I don't think it would be wise to barge up to the front door and knock," Frank commented.

"Right," Joe agreed. "We'll have to sneak in."

Ponsley shook his head. "You do as you please. I'll stay here."

"That's okay," Frank told him. "Joe, why don't you park behind that pile of rocks over there so the car will be out of sight."

Joe did and the boys got out, leaving Ponsley huddled in the back seat. The three youths headed for a point well to the right of the gateway. The fence was made up of five taut wire strands.

When they reached the gate, Frank and Joe got

down on their hands and knees and crawled under the lowest strand. Chet followed, but the wire caught him in the back. "I can't move!" he muttered to his friends.

"We'll get you loose," Frank whispered. "Just a minute!" Bracing himself with his feet, he lifted the taut wire as far as he could. Joe took hold of Chet's collar and tugged it. The wire released the boy, who shot forward on his face into the sandy soil on the opposite side of the fence.

"Okay, let's go!" Frank said.

"Wait. I lost a shoe!" Chet pleaded.

Joe slapped his forehead. "What a time to pick!" He felt around in the darkness, found the shoe, and pushed it into Chet's hand. "Tie it right this time," he warned. "You'll run like a lame duck with one shoe on and one off.

Chet did and the boys slipped from the fence across the yard to the lighted window, which was open halfway. Carefully stationing themselves in the darkness to one side of the light, they peered into the room.

A sofa stood against the wall, facing a big sideboard holding a number of decanters. In one corner a roll-top desk was open, revealing a series of pigeonholes filled with documents.

Six men sat around a table. Frank craned his head to get a better look at them. Then he whispered excitedly, "There's Tinted Glasses!"

"And Salty, the friendly sailor who almost killed

us with his cargo!" Joe added. "And there's the guy who tried to scare us away from Cutler Ranch!"

One of the men spoke, addressing Tinted Glasses. "I've got to hand it to you, Stiller. Everything's worked out just as you said it would."

Stiller nodded. "Sure, Bruno. But it would be better if Salty had picked the Hardys off on the dock!"

"I 'ad them set up," Salty declared. "They were lucky to get out of the way when I dropped that bale on them!"

"Well, make sure you carry out your assignments without any slip-ups in the future!"

"Sure I will," Salty said sullenly. "It's my neck as well as yours, you know."

"The next job is the most important of all," Stiller continued. "It's the last one. And everything's riding on it."

"I'll be glad when it's over," Bruno declared. "I want to get back to Wisconsin."

Stiller nodded. "I feel the same way. I'm tired of trailing the Hardys halfway around the world."

Salty chuckled. "Me, I'm luckier than you Yanks. Australia's 'ome to me."

Stiller frowned. "Your captain doesn't suspect you, does he?"

"No danger, mate. When you led the 'ardys down to the docks and tipped me the wink, I just slipped ashore long enough to get 'em off your back and set 'em up for the kill. All the skipper knows is, I'm an able seaman what knows 'ow to off-load cargo."

The door from the hall opened and a man and woman came in. The man was burly with long arms and large hands. The woman was short and dark with an intense expression. Both looked pleased as they shut the door.

Stiller addressed the man, "Well, Cutler, have you got the final marching orders for us?"

"I sure have," Cutler grinned. "I've just been on the phone to Sydney. We're to finish the job tonight!"

CHAPTER XIII

Daring Escape

"You finally got clearance to dump him in the Outback?" Bruno said. "Good. The desert will take care of him."

Stiller gave a wolfish grin. "That's right," he chortled. "It's as lethal as Death Valley back home in California."

"Dr. Jenson will never see the Firebird fly," Mrs. Cutler smirked.

"Right. The boss will come here to extract the missing information, then we'll dump him out among the snakes and lizards and leave the sun to finish the job."

The seedy man from Alice Springs shook his head doubtfully. "I'm not so sure that we'll be home free after the job," he spoke up. "I don't like the idea of the Hardys being in Alice Springs. I tried to scare them off when they started to get nosy, but we can't be sure it worked."

Cutler frowned. "Too bad this cowboy had to open his mouth about the ranch," he muttered.

"Well, they can't come out here to tonight," the seedy man went on. "I called the car rental agency and they were all out of transportation. But the Hardys just might show up here in a day or two and snoop around."

"By that time we'll be rid of Jenson," Stiller assured him. "And we'll destroy any incriminating evidence before tomorrow morning. I agree. We can't be careful enough. These guys are pretty smart. I still don't know how they got out of the Australian Arms Hotel without our seeing them!"

"And what gave them the idea to come to Alice Springs?" Bruno asked. "I know Jenson had no chance to leave word when Jim and I took him out of that fleabag hotel on Wallaby Drive. He was so doped he couldn't have written his own name, even if he had had a piece of paper."

"Maybe they just guessed," Bruno suggested.

"I don't know," Cutler said. "I have a bad feeling about this. Stiller, you'd better burn the lists of clients. The stuff about our previous kidnappings and the smuggling job could send us all up for life. Also, for as long as we're still here, we'll post a guard down at the road."

The Hardys listened outside the window with bated breath. Chet felt a cramp in one of his legs. He turned to place his weight on the other leg, stepped on a twig, and made a slight rustling noise.

Those inside looked in the direction of the sound. "What's going on?" Cutler snarled.

"Maybe someone's outside the window!" Mrs. Cutler cried. "Somebody might be spying on us!"

She rushed across the room to the window, while the boys ducked around the corner in the nick of time. Mrs. Cutler lifted the lamp and thrust it through the opening. Leaning out, she surveyed the area for a minute or two. Finally she pulled her head in, put the lamp down, and said, "Nobody's there. It must have been the wind blowing through the bushes."

The boys tiptoed back to the window as Cutler turned toward the gang. "What about our new man—the one guarding Jenson?"

"He's okay," Bruno declared. "I recruited him myself."

The boys felt their hearts pounding with fear as they listened to the criminals. Frank plucked Joe's and Chet's sleeves and motioned to them to move back from the window. They stopped near the fence where they had sneaked in.

"We've got to help Dr. Jenson!" Frank urged.

"How?" Chet queried. "We don't know where they're holding him. Could be anywhere in the farmhouse from the basement to the attic."

"We'll have to climb into the house and search it," Joe suggested.

Frank agreed. "Let's case the place and see if there's a way in. I tell you what. I'll scout the fence and see if there's an escape route. You two circle the ranch house in opposite directions and check the windows and doors. We'll meet here in a few minutes and compare notes."

"Right," Joe said. "Come on, Chet."

The pair went off into the darkness while Frank walked up to the fence and began following the strands of wire to guide himself around the perimeter of the yard. About every twenty-five feet he came to a post, but there was no break in the fence until he reached the gate in front. It was fastened by a chain and a padlock, but no guard was at the gate as yet.

"They must think no one but the gang will ever get out here," he thought. He continued around the fence to the place where they had sneaked in.

Joe, meanwhile, had gone to the left of the house. His path took him to a cellar door, a sloping wooden oblong obviously covering a small flight of stairs to the basement. Taking hold of the metal handle, Joe strove to lift the door. It was locked!

Farther on he passed a pickup truck and a station wagon. Noting that the keys were in both, he reflected, "These guys must really feel safe. Wouldn't it be something if the crooks' cars were stolen!"

Chet circled the house around the right side. He tried the dark lower windows only to find that they would not move. Then he stepped back for a view of the upper windows, which were inaccessible from the ground. "Not even a corner drainpipe to climb," he thought, disappointed.

Moving on, he met Joe sneaking toward him. Consulting in whispers, they decided to join Frank at the fence.

"If we can get Jenson out," Frank reported, "we'd better make a run for it down the road. Otherwise we could get lost in the desert."

"We may not be able to get him out," Chet said. "The ranch is buttoned up."

"I think the cellar door is our best bet," Joe stated. "Maybe we can spring the lock while they're all in the front room."

Frank nodded. "And then we'll have to jump the guy guarding Jenson before he can alert the gang. Let's hope it works!"

The three crept stealthily back to the house, edged around to the cellar door, and tried to wedge it open. Suddenly an uncanny scream made their hair stand on end!

"What's that?" Chet gasped.

A cat raced past, pursued by another. Noisily they vanished into the bushes and the boys breathed in relief.

"Wow!" Frank whispered. "They nearly gave me heart failure!"

The boys started to work on the cellar door once again. Joe took out a small set of pocket tools he carried for such emergencies, slipped the end of a tiny chisel between the edge of the door and the jamb, and levered skillfully until the spring of the lock snapped back. Elated, he began to lift the door.

A sound came from the rear of the ranch house, and Joe immediately eased the cellar door down into place again. The boys sprang up, pressed themselves flat against the wall, and froze as the back door opened.

Cutler came out on the patio. He held a flashlight in his hand and played it over the yard from the fence to the house. Foot by foot the light advanced across the ground to the cellar door. The boys stood stock-still, not daring to move a muscle! Now the beam shone inches from Chet's shoes, moving toward him!

At the last moment it wavered to one side because Mrs. Cutler emerged from the house and joined her husband on the patio. "What was that screeching sound?" she demanded.

"That's what I'm trying to find out," Cutler replied. He flipped the beam from the ground to the bushes, barely missing Chet's belt buckle.

Suddenly two pairs of eyes gleamed through the bushes and one of the cats began to growl.

"Only a couple of cats," Cutler informed his wife. "Nothing to worry about." He snapped the flashlight off and they went back inside.

Chet let out a sigh of relief. "Boy, that was a close call. I thought we were goners for sure!"

"What was that screeching sound?"
Mrs. Cutler demanded.

"If he'd aimed that flashlight a little higher," Joe whispered back, "he could have taken our pictures."

"There's no time to lose," Frank warned. "Let's make sure they're all in the front room. If one of them is prowling around, we're in trouble."

He led the way to the lighted window, where they could see that the Cutlers and gang members were assembled.

"Good," Frank declared. "We can go in——"

Wham! A window slammed over their heads and two men leaped down toward them from the darkness above. Instinctively the boys flattened themselves out against the wall. The men hurdled clear over them, hit the ground, jumped to their feet, and ran to the station wagon.

The Hardys got a good look at one man's face in the light from the window and recognized him from his photo. He was Dr. Jenson!

They could not see the other man's face, but as he jumped his hand caught the light from the room and sparkling red rays were reflected from a large ring on his finger.

"That must be Mike Moran!" Frank gasped.

CHAPTER XIV

Frank Foils the Gang

A TUMULT of furious screaming and shouting broke out in the ranch house.

"The room is empty!" Cutler yelled at the top of his voice. "They're gone—both of 'em!"

"Catch them!" Mrs. Cutler screeched savagely. "Don't let them get away!"

"We'll head 'em off!" Stiller shouted. "Put on the searchlight so we can see 'em!"

A moment later a beam of yellow light from a lookout post on the roof cut through the darkness. It picked up Jenson and Moran as they jumped into the station wagon. Moran started the car. The engine turned over—and died!

Shots rang out and bullets flew toward the station wagon, clanging off fenders and hub caps. One shattered the rear window as the men rushed out with Stiller in the lead. They pounded across the yard toward the fugitives.

Moran desperately turned the key in the starter

again. This time the engine came to life. He shifted gears, and the vehicle moved off just as Stiller grabbed the door handle on the driver's side. He glared angrily at the two men inside. He reached for the steering wheel and struggled with Moran for control, but Moran held on with an iron grip.

Stiller was dragged for about ten yards before losing his hold and falling off. He somersaulted in the dust and landed flat on his back. Cursing furiously, he got to his feet. The gang rushed up. Those who carried guns opened fire, but the station wagon was far ahead, moving quickly toward the gate.

"They'll have to stop!" Stiller snarled. "The gate's chained!"

The criminals ran as fast as they could, while the searchlight focused on the speeding station wagon. Moran stepped on the gas and smashed into the gate, causing it to splinter under the impact. The vehicle plowed through, carrying broken boards with it, and disappeared down the road.

Frank, Joe, and Chet observed the escape after sneaking to a corner of the ranch house from which they had a view of the gate. They felt like cheering when they saw the station wagon vanish into the darkness.

"They got away!" Chet chortled.

Joe shook his head. "Those guys'll go after them in the pickup unless we act fast!" He ran

to the truck, followed by Frank and Chet, leaned
in, and snatched the keys from the dashboard.
"That'll stop 'em!" He grinned.

"They may have another set of keys," Frank
said. "Better let the air out of this tire." He tried
to unscrew the valve cap, but it refused to budge.

Taking out his penknife, Frank gouged its
point into the rubber and began carving a small
slit in the tire sidewall until air leaked out with a
low hissing sound.

"Look out!" Joe warned. "They're coming!"

The boys melted into the darkness and hid
behind tall shrubs.

"We'll take the pickup and go after Jenson and
Moran," Stiller ordered. "Don't stand there! Get
in. I'll drive!"

As his henchmen obeyed, he squeezed behind
the wheel and reached for the keys. His fingers
hit an empty keyhole on the dashboard.

"My keys are gone!" he exploded. "Who took
'em? Which of you guys has been fooling around
this heap? Fork the key over!"

Each one denied knowing anything about the
key. Finally Bruno fished his own key from his
pocket and gave it to Stiller.

"No use arguing about it, boss," he said. "They
got a head start on us. We'll have to move if we
want to catch up."

Muttering to himself, Stiller turned on the ignition and the pickup took off with a roar. But
by this time the leaking tire had gone completely

flat. The rapidly whirling wheel bumped and clattered loudly over the rough ground, throwing the flattened tire casing halfway off the rim.

The truck lurched and jounced crazily from side to side while Stiller fought to bring it under control. One jolt broke the catch on the back gate, which dropped, and one of the men tumbled out. Finally Stiller brought the pickup to a stop.

"We've got a flat!" he fumed. "Salty, I thought you were gonna put new tires on so we could take Jenson for his ride!"

"I did, boss," Salty said defensively. "Look for yourself if you don't believe me."

"Don't worry. I will," Stiller retorted. He got out along with the others. The man who had fallen joined them, rubbing his shoulder.

"I'm okay," he said, "but those guys won't be when we nab 'em." He waved his fist.

"If you ask me, the tire was slashed!" fumed Bruno. "I'll bet Moran did it!"

"That's right," Stiller said. "He came out earlier to stretch his legs—or so he said. No doubt he punctured the tire while we weren't looking. He's the only one who could have. But he won't get away with it. We'll track him down."

"What I want to know," Salty interjected, "is 'ow Moran became a member of our group."

Bruno shrugged. "My fault. I met him at a soccer game in Sydney and he told me he wanted a job in the Outback because the law was after him. I fell for his story."

"You stupid jughead!" Stiller granted harshly. "We never should have listened to you."

"What do we do now?" Cutler asked.

"Change the tire. What else?" Stiller hissed. "Get busy, you guys!"

"The jack's in the station wagon," Bruno said sheepishly.

"What! You've got to be kidding!" Stiller screamed furiously. A shouting match followed until Salty brought it to an end. "Mates, I've got it!" he yelled.

"Got what?" Stiller demanded.

"The station wagon's low on petrol. I forgot to top 'er up yesterday. They'll get stuck somewhere between 'ere and Alice Springs!"

Stiller was thoughtful for a moment. "That's right. And all they can do is hide in the Outback, close to the road. We can get in touch with Bartel in the morning, and——"

"We won't have any trouble finding them, boss," Bruno added. "Don't worry about that."

"All right. But I don't want any more slip-ups. Let's set up guards for the rest of the night. We can't be sure that these snoopy boys won't show up sooner or later! Go inside and get some more ammunition. Then position yourselves around the property. We'll do two shifts."

The men agreed and everyone went inside. Frank pulled Joe and Chet by their jackets. "Let's get out of here, quick!"

CHAPTER XV

A Deadly Snake

THE boys raced through the darkness and wriggled through the fence. Then they ran around the rocks to the car. It appeared deserted as they approached.

"Where's Mr. Ponsley?" Chet puffed. "Do you think he got scared and ran off?"

"We'll have to stay and look for him," Joe said. "We can't just drive away and leave him behind!"

A loud noise interrupted him.

"No need to look for Mr. Ponsley," Frank observed. "He's here all right."

The boys peered through the window. Ponsley was sitting in the back seat with his hands crossed on his vest. His head was bent forward and his chin touched the enormous tie he wore. His mouth was open; and with every breath he snored.

Relieved to find he was still in the car, Frank, Joe, and Chet piled into the compact, then Frank took the wheel as they moved off. He drove carefully, not daring to use his lights until they were around the rocks and well down the road.

"We're safe now," Frank said, snapping on the headlights and stepping on the gas.

"As long as our car doesn't conk out," Chet stated. "I'll give three cheers when we get to Alice Springs."

"First we've got to find Jenson and Moran," Frank reminded him.

They came to a rough part of the road and jounced up and down over rocks and deep potholes. Frank shifted into low gear to maneuver past the worst spots. The jolting ride brought Ponsley awake with a start. He raised his head and looked around. "Where are we?" he demanded irritably.

"On the Cutler road," Frank replied.

Ponsley became peevish. "Well, you are driving this car as if you were riding a bronco at the rodeo."

"Can't help it," Frank said. "The Cutlers never built a paved highway for visitors to drive to their ranch."

Joe turned around and addressed their companion. "Mr. Ponsley, did you notice anything after we left you in the car?"

Ponsley covered a yawn with his hand. "What do you mean?" he asked.

"The station wagon. Did it keep on going down the road past the rocks?"

"What station wagon?" Ponsley inquired. "I know nothing about a station wagon."

Frank was incredulous. "You mean a station wagon crashed through a board fence only a few yards from where you were and you didn't hear anything?"

"I don't recall a thing between the time you left and just now, when you woke me up."

Frank increased speed as they reached a better stretch of the road. "Unbelievable!" He chuckled.

"Why are you going so fast?" Ponsley complained.

Joe explained that they had to get safely away from the gang of crooks at the Cutler Ranch.

Ponsley became cross. "I should think we are far enough away to slow down. I don't like being in an automobile at high speeds."

Frank turned onto the main road and increased his speed. "We have another reason for making time, Mr. Ponsley," he declared.

"Oh, what's that?"

"We're trying to catch Dr. Jenson and Mike Moran!"

Ponsley's mouth dropped open as the meaning of the statement sank in. The boys took turns describing events at the Cutler Ranch leading up to the climax, when Jenson and Moran leaped from the window of the house and fled in the station wagon.

"How did you know the man with Jenson was Michael?" he spluttered.

"He was wearing a ring with a red stone," Joe said. "It reflected in the light from the house."

Ponsley became excited. "Then it must be Michael! Frank, speed up! Catch the station wagon!"

Frank kept the gas pedal flat on the floor as the car raced forward. But trouble was in store. Several miles farther on, the car suddenly stalled. Lacking proper tools and light to work by, the boys puttered over the engine a long time before discovering that the distributor cap had sprung loose.

Later, after resuming their journey, they sighted distant figures silhouetted on the skyline. Ponsley insisted that they stop and investigate. The figures turned out to be wild aborigines hunting at night. Returning wearily to the car, they continued southward to Alice Springs.

Dawn began to break. Shafts of sunlight glanced from the desert in shimmering rays. Near the Sandover River, a group of kangaroos bounded away, and a rabbit scooted across the road, seeking safety in scrub vegetation.

Then something caught Joe's eye up ahead. "The station wagon!" he exclaimed.

Frank hit the brakes and brought the car to a stop behind the vehicle they had been chasing. Rocks and gullies extended on both sides of the road.

"Salty was right," Frank said. "They must have run out of gas."

Ponsley got out of the car as fast as he could. "Michael, Michael!" he called out.

There was no reply. Ponsley groaned. "They're gone!"

"The keys are still here," Joe pointed out.

Chet squeezed into the front seat, turned on the ignition, and glanced at the dashboard dials. "The gas needle's down to empty," he confirmed.

"Then they must be somewhere near here," Ponsley said hopefully. "But where?"

"Let's see if we can find their footprints and follow them," Frank suggested.

The four walked around the station wagon, but the terrain was too rocky for footprints.

"It's no use," Joe finally said. "We can't tell which way they went."

The boys shaded their eyes with their hands and scanned the horizon. Ponsley sat down on a boulder. Not a sound broke the silence of the desert, and not a movement could be seen among the rocks.

Joe was about to say something when he looked in Ponsley's direction and stopped short. Their friend was staring down toward his left hand, which was hidden by the boulder on which he sat. He looked deathly pale, his eyes bulged with fear, and a trickle of sweat rolled down his face. He seemed to have stopped breathing.

Joe stepped slowly around to see what was wrong. He noticed an Australian brown snake, about five feet long, coiled behind the boulder!

The snake's neck arched in the air. Flashing wicked fangs only inches from Ponsley's hand, the serpent swayed menacingly back and forth, hissing ferociously.

Ponsley was mesmerized by the venomous creature. He sat as if turned to stone, too terrified to move.

Cautiously, to avoid startling the snake and causing it to strike at Ponsley's hand, Joe gave a danger signal to Frank and Chet. Responding, they moved up, and were horrified when they realized that Ponsley was in danger.

Chet picked up a dried branch, evidently blown from a far-off straggle of gum trees, made a wide circle, came up behind the snake, and brushed the sand with the stick. With blinding speed, the snake whirled and sank its fangs into the wood!

Frank and Joe instantly grabbed Ponsley and pulled him away from the boulder. He trembled and gasped for breath. Chet stepped back, dragging the snake, which maintained its grip on the stick.

"Look!" Joe cried suddenly.

Between the serpent's coils gleamed a piece of metal. When the snake released the stick and slithered off among the rocks, Joe retrieved the object, a key chain with the initial M on it.

"That's probably Michael's!" Ponsley exclaimed. "He must have dropped it here!"

"Most likely on the way up this gully," Frank observed. "So that's where we go."

The gully led to a point where the rocks were taller and more spread out, with defiles leading in several directions. They halted, not knowing which way to take.

Frank cupped his hands around his mouth. "Mike Moran!" he shouted. "Come on out! We're friends!"

His words echoed among the rocks and then silence fell again.

Joe called, "Dr. Jenson! Dr. Jenson!"

Again silence. A small stone tumbled from one of the tall rocks. Looking up, the boys saw a figure vanish over the top.

"There they are!" Chet cried out.

The four climbed over a pile of rocks and reached the top just in time to see the figure jump down on the other side and run into a defile.

"They think we're Stiller and company," Joe said. "They won't come out."

"You follow them," Frank replied. "I'll cut them off."

Noting that the defile curved around in a semicircle, he scrambled down the pile of rocks, turned left, and met Moran and Jenson running through toward him!

Jenson was a slight, scholarly-looking man. Moran appeared to be the outdoor type, and he assumed a boxer's stance as soon as he saw Frank.

"Relax, Mike," Frank told him. "We're not in

league with the Cutlers. Those crooks are a long way from here."

Just then the others came up. Ponsley hastened forward and cried, "Michael! Michael!"

Moran stared at him in utter astonishment. "Mr. Ponsley, what are you doing here?"

"And who are these boys?" Jenson put in.

"Friends!" Ponsley said. Then he explained how they happened to be searching for Moran and Jenson.

When Ponsley mentioned that Michael had been accused of tipping off two bank robbers about the Mid-County Bank's alarm system, Moran shook his head in disbelief. "Dad needn't have worried about that. The alarm system they've got now is totally different from the one in use when I worked there. I know nothing about the present system."

"Can you prove that?" Joe asked.

"Sure. The old system had a number of flaws. I know because I checked it out. The manager called in a security engineering firm to install a new one. The job hadn't been finished when I left. The records will back me up on that."

"So the two men who were arrested must have been trying to frame you to cover up for someone else," Frank reasoned.

"You bet they were!" said Mike.

Ponsley heaved a sigh of relief now that he knew the senator's son could be cleared. The conversation reminded Frank of something. "You spoke about a bank employee named Thurbow, who helped to throw suspicion on Mike," he said to Ponsley. "What's his job there?"

"Security guard, I believe."

"Any idea what he looks like?"

"I have," Mike broke in. "He's a stocky, red-haired guy with a broken nose. I never did like him."

Frank turned to his brother. "Remember the man who was in the chemistry shop talking to Mr. Oakes when we ordered that methyl yellow?"

Joe's eyes widened and he snapped his fingers. "Holy smoke, you're right! It was a chunky red-head! I remember wondering if he might be a pro boxer with that broken nose. That must have been Thurbow."

"Check! Mr. Oakes told us he was talking to a security guard when the mistake occurred. I'll bet Thurbow switched the methyl yellow with his own bottle of liquid gas."

"Probably because he heard at the bank that Senator Moran planned to call us in on the case."

The two boys told their listeners about their accident with the tear gas.

Later Ponsley inquired reproachfully, "Michael, why did you leave your home like that?"

"I wanted to see the world without my father's help. I decided to stop being Senator Moran's son for a while and try to make it on my own."

"How did you get involved with the Stiller gang?" Frank asked.

"I met Bruno at a soccer match in Sydney. He said he was from a ranch in the Outback and when I told him I was looking for a job, he hired me. I didn't know anything about the illegal operations till I got to Cutler Ranch."

Frank remembered that Bruno said Moran had claimed the police were after him, but decided not to mention it at this point.

"Mike was already there when they dragged me out of the hotel in Sydney," Jenson took up the story. "They drugged me to make it easier, but I heard them mention Alice Springs and wrote the letters AL S on the door. Did you read my message?"

"Sure did," Frank said. "But tell me, why did you pick that fleabag hotel in the first place?"

"I had a feeling I was being followed. I had reservations at the Australian Arms, but I took a taxi at the airport and told the driver to take me to the opposite part of town. Unfortunately, it didn't help. They found me anyway."

"So after that you two met at the Cutler Ranch," Joe said to Mike.

"Right. That's where Bruno took me. He told me to guard Dr. Jenson when they brought him in. Bruno handed me a rifle and ordered me to see that Dr. Jenson stayed put in the upstairs room until his fate had been decided. When it seemed that they were going to drop him in the Outback, we escaped through the window. We didn't see you fellows. It was too dark. I had been in the yard, and I knew the keys were in the station wagon. That's why we used it for our break-out. We drove till the gas ran out."

"Then we hid in the rocks," Jenson continued. "When you came along and stopped behind the station wagon, we thought you were Stiller and his henchmen."

"That's why we hid even deeper," Moran said. "By the way, how did you know which way we had gone?"

"We found this at the head of the gully," Joe replied. He handed the key chain to Mike Moran.

Moran took it and put it in his pocket. "I must have dropped it after we got out of the car. Good thing you found it!"

"Thank the deadly snake, Mike," Joe quipped.

"What's that again?"

Joe described the incident of the hissing ser-pent.

Moran became solemn. "I'm sorry you were in so much danger, Mr. Ponsley."

The latter held up his hand. "Think nothing of it, Michael. I have found you, and nothing else concerns me at this point."

Frank turned to Jenson. "Do you have any idea why the gang kidnapped you?"

"None at all. It's a mystery to me."

"Could they be agents of a foreign government?"

"They might," Jenson confessed. "Professor Young and I received several messages warning us not to test the Firebird Rocket. Certainly a foreign power might be involved. It might be a plot to hold up our space program."

A loud clatter broke out overhead and a helicopter zoomed through the sky. It was painted white, and bore no markings. The pilot made a wide circle around the two cars parked by the side of the road. Obviously interested in them, he returned for a second look.

"Chopper!" Chet cried. "If we can attract the pilot's attention, maybe he'll pick us up. Come on, we'll send him an SOS before he flies off!"

The rotund youth ran down the gully and out into the open. The others followed on his heels. Chet began to wave his arms frantically.

"Chet, be careful!" Frank warned. "It could be Stiller and his gang!"

Chet ignored the warning. Exultantly he realized that the pilot had spotted the group. "He saw us and is coming down for us!"

The chopper swung low toward them. Then machine guns chattered! Bullets kicked up puffs of sand on the desert floor!

CHAPTER XVI

Helicopter Hunt

"RUN BEHIND the rocks!" Joe shouted. "We're clay pigeons out here in the open!"

He raced back up the gully, followed by the others. The helicopter pursued them, its machine guns spraying bullets at their heels. They circled around the rocks until they found sanctuary under an overhanging ledge. Baffled by this obstruction, the chopper pilot hovered in the sky like a hawk waiting for its prey to emerge from a hole in the ground.

The six fugitives crept into a large cave at the end of the ledge. Ponsley sank down and mopped his brow with his handkerchief. Jenson sat down beside him. The Hardys, Chet, and Moran peered through the mouth of the cave at their enemy overhead.

"We're safe for the moment," Frank said. "But the helicopter will keep hunting us."

Ponsley turned pale and gasped, "Then why are we staying in here? We'll be trapped!"

"We can't get back to the car while the chopper's in the air," Frank replied. "Let's wait until the pilot lands."

As if in response to his words, the whirlybird began to circle lower and lower, finally settling on the desert in a cloud of dust. The door opened and Stiller jumped out, followed by Bruno and another man. They both carried machine guns.

"Run before they find us!" Frank called out to his companions. "Now!"

He was first out of the cave. Chet, Moran, Jenson, and Ponsley came after, with Joe at the end of the line to make sure no one was left behind. They took the reverse direction along the overhanging ledge, just making it around the rocks before a volley of shots rang out as the gang spotted them.

Quickly they ran down the gully to the car and piled into it. The gang pounded after them.

Frank took the wheel, and the car roared off amid a hail of bullets fired by Stiller and his henchmen.

"Anybody get hit?" Joe asked anxiously.

He felt relieved when everyone reassured him that he had not. Peering through the back window, he saw the gang turn and run up the gully.

"They're going back to the chopper!" he said grimly. "That means they'll be after us again."

"Oh, no!" Ponsley protested. He was squeezed into one corner of the car with his elbows pressed tightly against his sides. "It's bad enough riding like this! I can't breathe!"

"It'll get worse in a minute," Joe predicted.

He was right. The helicopter appeared in the sky and thundered after the car. One of the machine guns opened up again, kicking up sand behind the rear wheels of the speeding vehicle.

Frank swerved sharply from one side of the road to the other, presenting a moving target to the gunner. Reaching a row of hills, he dodged into them. He sped in and out among them, rocking the car violently as he took sharp corners on two wheels. The brakes squealed.

"We'll never get out of this alive!" Ponsley lamented. "We're done for!"

"Not yet!" Frank vowed. "We'll give them a run for their money!"

The hills ended, and the car was forced back onto the road through the Outback. The chopper resumed the chase, throwing a moving shadow on the earth like that of a giant prehistoric bird flapping through the early morning sunlight.

Frank raced down the road. "How long can that guy keep missing us with his burp gun?" he wondered.

"They're trying to draw a bead on us," Joe warned. "Here they come. Everybody duck!"

"Duck?" Ponsley quavered. "I can't even move!"

"What's that?" Chet cried, pointing down the road to a speck on the horizon that was growing larger by the second.

"It's a car!" Frank exclaimed.

The two vehicles raced toward one another. Frank blinked his headlights on and off as a signal to the other driver that he was in trouble.

"I hope he can help us!" Chet said.

"He sure will!" Frank replied. "That's a police car!"

The helicopter pilot, recognizing the police insignia, veered off and clattered away, vanishing in the distance. Frank drew to a stop, and so did the patrol car. Two officers got out.

"Boy, are we glad to see you!" Frank exclaimed.

"What's the matter?" asked one of the officers.

Frank introduced himself and his companions, then explained that the helicopter had been chasing and firing at them.

"Why were the men in the chopper after you?"

Joe and Chet took turns describing what had occurred since they arrived at the Cutler Ranch. Moran and Jenson added their testimony, and told how they happened to be at the ranch.

The policemen listened in amazement. "We saw the copter and heard the gunfire quite a distance away, but we couldn't figure out what was going on," said one officer.

His partner added, "We'll call for reinforcements and drive to the Cutler homestead immediately."

"But the chopper will get there before you," Frank pointed out.

"True. But it's too small to fly out that many people. We should be able to nab at least some of the gang."

The two officers got into their patrol car and started up the road through the Outback, while Frank and the others continued to Alice Springs. They drove straight to the rental agency and returned the car.

Ponsley was so stiff that he had to be pulled out of the back seat by Chet and the Hardys. "Oh, my aching back!" he complained. "Mike, why did you ever have to come to a place like this?"

"I like this country," Mike said with a grin. "What do we do next?"

"Fly back to America at once!" Ponsley declared. "Michael, your father can't wait to see you."

Moran nodded. "And I can't wait to see him and Mom."

"I'd better fly to Sydney to check in with the Australian authorities and confirm my clearance at Woomera," Dr. Jenson said.

Frank said, "And I think we should go with you in case the gang tries to kidnap you again. Until they're behind bars, I know Dad would want us to act as your bodyguards, Dr. Jenson."

The scientist smiled. "I'll be happy to have you. It makes me feel a lot safer."

On the plane to Sydney, Mike Moran told them about some of his experiences and how he had run out of money and accepted the job Bruno offered him.

"Did you tell him the police were after you?" Frank asked bluntly.

Mike stared at him for a moment. "No. Why do you ask?"

"Bruno said you did."

"You spoke to him?"

"No. We overheard him saying it."

"Well, it's not true."

Frank had doubts but changed the subject. "Now you can help your father in his political campaign," he suggested.

"I'll be glad to," Mike said. "After my experiences down under, politics will be a tame game. But that's all right. I don't want to get involved with any more criminals."

At the Sydney airport, Ponsley and Moran said good-by and went to catch a plane for the United States. The boys accompanied Dr. Jenson to police headquarters and then returned with him to the airport to await a flight to Adelaide, where they would transfer to another plane for the Woomera rocket station.

While they were sitting in the terminal, a voice announced over the loudspeaker: "Call for Joe Hardy! Call for Joe Hardy!"

"Who can that be?" Joe wondered.

"You'll find out when you answer," Chet said.

After checking with the information desk, Joe went to the designated phone booth and picked up the receiver. "Joe Hardy speaking."

"Listen, punk," growled a disguised voice, "you and your brother better get out of Australia! And take your fat friend with you—or all three of you will wind up in the hospital! Or in coffins!"

CHAPTER XVII

Woomera Welcome

JOE started to ask who the speaker was but the phone clicked off at the other end. Replacing the receiver, the boy returned to the others and quickly described the warning call.

"The helicopter gang knew we were with Dr. Jenson," Chet said. "They could have called ahead of us to alert another member. He may follow us, so we'd better be on our guard."

Frank nodded thoughtfully. "But do you know what this means? Unless they called their accomplice while they were still in the air, they escaped the police!"

"I'm going to get in touch with the Alice Springs police right away," Joe said and hurried off to a phone booth. He managed to reach the officer in charge. "Did you capture the Stiller gang?" he asked.

"No such luck. We found the Cutler station abandoned. Obviously other gang members arrived with cars to help evacuate everyone. So far we haven't traced the helicopter or its crew."

Joe groaned in disappointment. "Any clues in the house?"

"Nothing. It was cleaned out except for some fingerprints. There were a lot of ashes in the fireplace and bits of paper, but nothing conclusive. They obviously burned anything incriminating."

"And no hint to where they might have gone?"

"None. But we're working on the case and will find out sooner or later."

Joe thanked the officer and hung up. When he joined his brother and the others, they could tell from the expression on his face that something had gone wrong.

"The Cutler gang escaped?" Frank asked.

"Without a trace. They burned all the evidence and were gone when the police arrived."

"They must have been prepared even before the helicopter went off to chase us," Frank muttered.

"Do you think they'll make another attempt to kidnap Dr. Jenson?" Chet asked.

"It's possible. We have to be very careful."

The scientist turned pale when he heard that his captors were still at large. "I'm glad you fellows are with me," he said. "And I'll feel better yet once we get to Woomera. The security there is so tight, I doubt that any of the gang could get in."

His companions nodded, and they kept a sharp

eye out for anyone who might be following them. They boarded the plane without noticing anything suspicious.

The plane flew over the desolate terrain of Southern Australia, then made a big circle to the coast over Gulf St. Vincent and into Adelaide for a landing at the airport. There, a message was waiting for Dr. Jenson.

"Professor David Hopkins is here to meet me," he declared after reading the note.

"Dr. Jenson, who is this professor?" Frank asked. "Do you know him?"

"We can't take chances with strangers," Joe added.

Jenson laughed. "I've never met him, but I know he's a famous scientist. He's one of the experts I came to Australia to meet. Hopkins works out the astronomical tables for interplanetary probes and will help track the Firebird."

"The man who is meeting us here could be a phony," Frank objected.

"Don't worry," Dr. Jenson assured him. "I know what Hopkins looks like. I've seen several pictures of him."

"Good," Frank said. "I'd hate to walk into a trap."

Jenson led the way to the waiting room, looked around, then waved to a man sitting on a bench. It was obviously Hopkins. Frank was relieved by the gesture.

The scientist was a short-sighted individual

wearing steel-rimmed glasses. He came forward and introduced himself.

"Dr. Jenson, the Sydney police informed us that you were coming," he said. "I couldn't wait to see you, so I flew down to Adelaide. We're all so glad to hear that you survived your ordeal unharmed!"

"So am I," Jenson said with a smile. He shook Hopkins' hand, introduced the Hardys and Chet, and gave Hopkins a brief rundown on his escape from the Cutler Ranch. "The boys came along as my bodyguards," he concluded.

"That's a splendid idea in view of the danger," Hopkins declared emphatically. "Now then. We'll fly to Woomera in an official plane. The station's in the desert, where the rockets can be safely tested."

The plane was a medium-sized, propeller-driven craft, just large enough for them to squeeze in behind the pilot. After taking off, they headed northwest over Spencer Gulf and Port Augusta into a region of lakes that broke up the arid, sun-bitten terrain of western Australia.

After their long, cramped flight drew to an end, Hopkins pointed out the window and said, "This is the Woomera prohibited area. It's a very large tract of land, absolutely barred to visitors who don't have official permission to enter."

"I know why," Chet boasted. "Your rockets are top secret! Space probes! Spy-in-the-sky! All that hardware!"

Hopkins smiled. "You seem to know about this."

Chet puffed his chest out. "I built a rocket myself and won the high school science competition!"

The Australian smiled again. "Perhaps some day you'll be working here as a scientist."

Chet looked pleased. "I would——"

"We're about to land," the pilot interjected. He maneuvered the plane in line with the runway, set down the wheels, and taxied to the terminal. Hopkins oversaw his companions' clearance by the Woomera security staff, then took them in his car to their hotel.

"This town sprang up overnight," he said as they drove along. "Even the trees you see were planted. Now we have homes, apartments, swimming pools—everything from a post office to a hospital. We'll go out to the rocket range in the morning," he added upon drawing up to the curb to let his passengers out.

It was decided that Dr. Jenson would share his room with Chet for security reasons, and the Hardys asked for adjoining quarters. However, the night passed without an incident, and Hopkins picked them up, as promised, early next day.

They drove to the central installation and saw rockets of all sizes at launch sites. Some stood upright, ready to fly into orbit. Others were canted at an angle that would keep them from reaching outer space.

Hopkins took the boys into a building and led them to its main room, which contained rows of sensitive instruments. Scientists and technicians were seated at consoles, checking the readings. "This is the control room," he said, "and these instruments monitor our rockets."

A man in a white coat was bending over a telemetry computer. When he heard Hopkins' voice, he straightened up and looked around. The Hardys stared in surprise. He was Professor Young!

"Adrian!" Young exclaimed, stepping over and shaking Jenson's hand. "I'm so glad the Hardys found you! Good job!"

Frank and Joe smiled and Chet looked a little disappointed because he had not been mentioned.

"Well, I want to welcome all of you to Woomera," Young went on. "I came here to follow the Firebird flight because I was afraid you wouldn't make it!"

"I almost didn't," Jenson said, and told Young about his experiences since he was last heard from.

Young looked grim. "NASA will do everything to see that your kidnappers are brought to justice. Please give me all the details of your capture."

He questioned Jenson and the boys very closely for an hour. At the end, he said, "Adrian, I take it you still have no idea why the Stiller gang kidnapped you."

Jenson shook his head. "I wish I could tell you. But I can't."

"When Cutler and his men are found, they may talk," Frank suggested.

"Let's hope so!" Young declared fervently. He

invited Jenson to come into his office for a briefing about the Firebird. Then he turned to the boys. "While Dr. Jenson and I are talking, I'll bet I know what you fellows would like to do."

"I'd like to see a rocket launching!" Chet said.

"I figured that," Young said with a smile. "You're in luck. There will be one in about five minutes. Come along with me."

He escorted the boys to a special observation window through which they could see a huge missile poised on its launch pad. Then the two men disappeared while the Hardys and Chet waited expectantly, their eyes glued to the rocket.

The nose cone was painted dark green and the booster was white with the name *Wallaby* on it. A supporting gantry moved back, leaving the rocket standing by itself on the launch pad.

An Australian scientist came up to watch. "You're Americans, aren't you?" he asked.

Frank said they were.

"I thought so from hearing you speak. That rocket is named for a small kangaroo, the wallaby. It will put a weather satellite into orbit." He stood near them while preparations for the launching continued. At last everything was ready.

"Here we go!" Chet cried. "The countdown!"

A voice intoned the numbers: "Ten, nine, eight, seven, six, five, four, three, two, one, zero! Lift off!"

Exhaust gases poured out onto the launch pad in a dense white cloud. The rocket started straight up, slowly at first, then gathered momentum, and increased its speed. Soon it was hurtling through the sky high above the earth.

The scientists and technicians in the control room cheered loudly and the boys joined in.

"That's a beauty!" Joe said enthusiastically. "I hope she makes it into orbit!"

"So far, so good," reported Frank, who was following the flight through a pair of binoculars offered him by the Australian. "It looks like a perfect flight."

"I'll show you how perfect," the Australian said when the rocket had disappeared from view. He took them to a battery of instruments to check the moment the booster rocket fell away and the nose cone continued into orbit.

Young's voice sounded behind them. "Everything is going as planned. The flight is A-okay."

He and Jenson had come up without being noticed, and stood looking at the instruments over Frank's shoulder.

"It's an important flight for us," Jenson said. "The data it sends back will be used to plot the flight of the Firebird."

Everyone in the control room relaxed. They began to discuss the Firebird, its revolutionary nuclear engine, and the path it would take deep into space. Young showed the boys around, introducing them to Australians and Americans responsible for space programs conducted jointly by the two nations.

The rocket slowly started straight up.

Chet eagerly asked as many questions as he could think of and the scientists cooperated good-naturedly with the boy. Finally, in the late afternoon, the young detectives escorted Dr. Jenson back to their hotel. They had a pleasant dinner, then retired to their rooms. Before going to bed, Frank telephoned Alice Springs again.

"Any clues yet?" he asked the officer in charge.

"We found the helicopter abandoned in the Outback," was the reply. "It was registered in the name of Bartel. At this point we haven't been able to establish yet whether that's a fictitious name or not. But there's no trace of the gang."

"I was afraid of that," Frank said. Slowly he hung up and told Joe what the officer had reported.

"I just hope that dodging the police will take up all the gang's time and attention," Joe commented. "This way they won't be able to follow us."

Joe's hopes, however, were dashed the following morning when a loud knock sounded on the door. Dr. Jenson and Chet burst in. The scientist looked pale and shaken, and his hand trembled slightly as he held out a piece of paper to show the boys.

"This was slipped under the door of our room," he exclaimed. "They're going to kill me!"

CHAPTER XVIII

The Trap

FRANK and Joe stared at the message. It was pieced together with letters cut out of a newspaper, a method the crooks had used before, and read: THE FIREBIRD WILL DIE, AND SO WILL YOU!

"They haven't given up," Joe stormed. "And they know where we are. It looks as if security isn't tight enough, even here at Woomera!"

"Maybe Arthur can help," Jenson said. Suddenly he sounded tired and depressed.

"Look," Frank told him, "don't worry about the gang. That's what we're here for."

Jenson smiled wanly. "Okay, I'll let you worry. Do you think it's safe to go downstairs and have some coffee?"

The group went into the cafeteria, and less than an hour later the official limousine picked them up. They were driven to the rocket range, where they met Young in the laboratory.

He was agitated when he saw the note. "This is unbelievable!" he exploded. "But they won't get away with this. I won't let them!"

"You didn't get a note like this?" Frank inquired.

"No," Young said, and he turned pale. "Not yet."

"What are you doing for your own safety?" Joe added.

"I traveled with the two men who guarded me in Princeton," Young replied, "and we're sharing a room. That, of course, may not discourage the gang from coming after me, too."

"What are we going to do?" Jenson asked.

"I'll talk to the security people here and arrange for a hideout where the four of you can stay until the gang is captured," Young replied. "I'll figure out a way we can communicate with each other, and also request closer protection for myself. Just wait here while I make a few phone calls."

Young disappeared into his office and returned a short time later. "All set," he declared. "The private pilot who flew me here will take you to a safe place down in Port Augusta. No one will suspect you're there, and the local police will keep an eye on it. Please don't leave until I contact you."

Soon Jenson and the boys took off, and less than an hour later they landed at the Port Augusta airfield, where a car was waiting. The pilot himself drove them to a hotel on the outskirts of town. He pulled into the rear and backed up closely to the door.

The boys had noticed a large sign out front that read: CAPTAIN COOK'S FLAGSHIP. The ancient three-story building needed a coat of paint, the windows needed washing, and the lawn needed mowing.

"This is not exactly a first-class joint," Chet commented.

"Why did Professor Young send us to a place like this?" Joe wondered.

"Obviously he thinks no one would look here for an eminent scientist," Frank suggested.

They went in and found a surly clerk at the desk. He glowered at them as they signed the register, and told them their room was on the third floor.

"The only phone in the hotel is this one on the desk," he snapped. "You can have sandwiches from the kitchen. Water and ice are in the basement. Take the stairs up, and don't ask me if there's a lift. There isn't."

"He's about as friendly as that brown snake Ponsley met in the Outback," Frank said sarcastically as they climbed the stairs. Finding their door number, they entered a dusty room with four cots, and a window that was stuck. Joe and Chet had to force it up by pushing together.

Jenson looked around and sighed. "I hope we don't have to stay here very long."

"Stiller and his friends might be rounded up at

any time." Frank reassured him. "Then we can leave."

Joe punched one cot with his fist. "This'll be like camping out in the Bayport Woods," he grumbled.

Chet clicked his teeth. "I'm thirsty. I'll go get some ice water in the basement."

He went out, carrying a cracked jug that had been sitting on a small table. Joe locked the door and put the key on the bureau. Frank and Jenson sat down on two cots and discussed the situation, wondering what would come next. Suddenly the floorboards in the hall creaked and footsteps approached.

"I didn't think Chet would be back that fast," Joe said.

The steps came closer and stopped outside their door. However, the caller did not knock.

"Whoever's out there must be eavesdropping on us!" Jenson whispered nervously.

"Shhh!" Joe warned, putting his finger to his lips. He and Frank tiptoed over to the door. Joe stationed himself flat against the wall next to it, while Frank turned the knob quickly and flung the door open.

Outside stood the desk clerk!

"What's the idea of eavesdropping on us?" Frank demanded.

"Who's eavesdropping? I came up to tell you there's a phone call for Frank and Joe Hardy. You can take it at the desk."

"Then why didn't you knock?"

"I wanted to make sure no one was around. I was told to be cautious and not to draw attention to this room."

"That sounds reasonable," Jenson spoke up. "Arthur doesn't want anyone to know we're here. He's being careful."

"It's possible," Joe commented.

The desk clerk glared at them. "I delivered the message," he grated. "Now I've got other things to do." He walked out and disappeared down the hall. The Hardys followed him after warning Jenson to lock the door and not to open it for anyone except Chet until they returned.

"This call must be from Professor Young," Joe said as they descended the stairs. "Maybe the police caught the gang!"

They took the lower stairs two at a time and ran to the desk. The clerk was not in sight and the phone lay on its side off the hook.

Frank lifted the instrument to his ear and Joe stood close enough to listen in. "Hello?" Frank said.

A disguised voice replied, "Listen, Hardy! You and that stupid brother of yours don't seem to have sense enough to save yourselves, much less protect Jenson!"

"Who is this?" Frank demanded.

"The same person who called Joe Hardy at the Sydney airport."

"What are you calling about now?"

"You all disregarded my warning," the man retorted. "I gave you a chance to save your necks
and you didn't take it. You decided to stay in Australia. All right, now you'll stay permanently. Six
feet under!"

The man continued his threats. Frank put his
hand over the mouthpiece and whispered, "Joe,
do you recognize his voice?"

"It's disguised," Joe replied. "I don't know him
from Adam."

Frank removed his hand from the telephone
and said, "Who's going to make us stay permanently?"

The man hung up without answering and the
Hardys stared at one another in puzzlement.

"This means we can't stay here either," Frank
said. "We'd better phone Professor Young!"

Joe called and described the threat. Young was
disturbed. "Good heavens!" he exclaimed. "I'll
phone my pilot to go back for you right away. He's
still in Port Augusta. All of you had better go to
the airfield with him before the gang gets to the
hotel!"

"Will do, professor," Joe said. "See you later."
He and Frank hurried upstairs and knocked on
the door of their room. There was no answer. Joe
tried the knob and found the door was locked.

"Dr. Jenson!" the Hardys called in unison.

Frank looked grim. "Something's happened.
We'll have to break in!"

He kicked the door until a panel splintered under the impact. Reaching through, he turned the key in the lock and pushed the door open. The room was empty!"

Footsteps in the hall made them whirl around. Chet came in, carrying his jug. "The ice water comes out in a trickle," he complained. "Say, what have you done to the door?"

"Dr. Jenson is gone!" Frank said. "Did you see him downstairs?"

"Or anybody else?" Joe added.

Chet shook his head. "I was all by my lonesome."

"There's only one other way out," Frank said. "Through the window!"

The Hardys rushed over and saw that a sheet had been torn into strips and knotted together to form a rope. One end was tied to a radiator. The other dangled over the windowsill to the ground.

"Dr. Jenson got out through the window!" Frank exclaimed. "We've got to catch him!"

"But why would he do that?" Chet asked.

"I have no idea. All I know is that we must get him!" Frank said. He left a bill on the dresser for the damage to the door, then gripped the improvised rope, and shinned to the ground with the celerity of a squirrel. Joe followed at the same speed, then looked up.

Chet was hesitating.

"Hurry up or stay behind!" Joe urged.

Faced with the choice, Chet climbed down. He got hold of the torn sheet, and squeezed through the window, shutting his eyes tight. He dangled over empty space. "It's a three-story drop," he quavered.

"Slide down! Let gravity take over," Joe advised. "You'll make it in no time."

Chet had almost reached the bottom when one end of the torn sheet snapped. He plummeted down with a loud yell. Frank grabbed his shoulders and Joe caught his legs, and the three ended in a tangle on the ground.

"Good show!" said a familiar voice behind them as they struggled to their feet. The boys froze. It was Stiller! He and his gang had them surrounded! In the background, Salty was guarding Jenson, whose hands were tied.

"We laid a trap," Stiller smirked, "and the smart Hardys walked right into it!"

Frank realized what had happened. "You guys must have sneaked in the back way before we ever got that call. And somehow you fooled Dr. Jenson into opening the door while your confederate kept us talking down at the hotel desk."

"That's right." Stiller gloated. "We pounded on the door and pretended you two had had an accident. When Jenson opened, we grabbed him and left that knotted sheet dangling out the window before we ducked down the back stairs again. One of my men actually climbed down the sheet so he could lock the door from the inside. You fools fell for the trick and plopped right into our arms!"

Jenson and the young detectives were taken to two parked cars. At the wheel of one was the hotel desk clerk!

"So you're in the gang, too," Frank accused him.

The clerk grinned. "I am now," he said as the captives were pushed into the cars. "It pays well."

"Where are you taking us?" Frank asked Bruno, who sat next to him.

"Shut up!" his guard answered and jabbed him viciously in the side with his elbow.

Frank winced in pain and asked no more questions. The cars were driven to an abandoned warehouse several blocks away. It was a five-story building. Most of the windows were broken or boarded up.

The gang marched the captives inside and up a flight of dark stairs to the loft at the top. One man was posted to guard them while his companions left. About an hour later, the other crooks returned with a new prisoner. The boys gasped as they recognized him.

"Professor Young!" they cried out in disbelief.

Dr. Jenson stared at his partner. "Arthur! So they've got you too! How on earth did it happen?"

"A fake phone call right after I talked to Joe," Young replied. "The caller pretended to be with the Port Augusta police. He said they had a line on the gang and were ready to close in. He wanted me to fly here immediately to help identify them as soon as they were captured. But the person who

met me at the airfield when I landed turned out
to be my kidnapper."

"We tricked you as easily as we tricked your
friends here," Stiller sneered at him.

"What are you going to do with us?" Chet
asked.

"Finish you off, what else!"

CHAPTER XIX

The Rope Trick

FRANK and Joe looked at each other. Both realized that they would have to fight their way out. Frank counted the gang members that were in the room with them. Stiller, Salty, Bruno, the hotel clerk, and another man that Stiller had called Bartel. "The owner of the helicopter, no doubt," Frank thought and wondered vaguely where the Cutlers were.

The Hardys knew they had a chance to subdue their adversaries if Young helped. Jenson was handcuffed. With a yell to Joe and Chet, Frank threw himself on the man nearest him. Joe did the same, and Chet, who caught on immediately, flattened Salty with a blow to the chin.

The next few minutes were bedlam. Stiller attacked Frank, while Joe took Cutler with a flying tackle. Young seemed frozen and stood stock-still as Chet seized Bruno in a tight headlock. Even Dr.

Jenson got into the fray and tripped a couple of men who were about to attack the Hardys.

Just then Mr. and Mrs. Cutler arrived. Cutler threw himself into the fight, turning the odds heavily against the young detectives. One by one the boys were overpowered. Jenson was lying on the floor, and Young stood frozen, as if in shock.

"Let's tie 'em up," Cutler panted, and his wife went to get a supply of rope. Soon the boys and the two scientists had their hands bound behind their backs and their ankles tied. Then the gang filed out of the room.

"They won't be here long," Stiller muttered to Salty on the way out. "And I'll be glad when we're rid of them for good!"

The door slammed shut, a key turned in the lock, and the men went downstairs. Slowly their footsteps died away.

"Work on the ties," Frank advised his companions. "If we slide up to one another, we can try to use our fingers to loosen each other's ropes. Here, watch me." He rolled up to Joe and wriggled until the two lay next to each other, facing opposite directions. Then, with great patience, he worked on his brother's bonds. Jenson and Young followed suit, while Chet waited until Frank had untied Joe and was able to help him. A half hour later everyone was free. Dr. Jenson sat down in a corner with his head in his hands. He had gone through so much already that he had lost all hope.

Young, however, had overcome his panic and

tried to encourage his partner. "Adrian, don't give up yet. Perhaps we'll all be saved, and the Firebird will be launched on schedule. Let's go over those final calculations again so we'll be prepared."

"You really think there's a chance?" Jenson asked, wanting to believe there was.

"There always is," Young assured him. "Here, I have some paper in my pocket. Let's write down the equations."

Frank, Joe, and Chet, meanwhile, looked around the huge bare dusty room, seeking some means of escape. Aside from the door, which had been locked, the only other way out seemed to be through a single unboarded window. Its pane was cracked and the frame broken, but Chet managed to open the sash far enough to peer out.

"We can't climb down," he informed his friends. "Too high up."

Frank and Joe joined him and saw that the wall descended five stories without offering a toehold anywhere along the way. Nor was there any possibility of climbing to the roof, ten feet above.

"Are you sure?" Young called out, interrupting his discussion with Dr. Jenson.

"Positive," Chet confirmed. He craned out as far as possible, surveying the wall to the left and right.

"Maybe if we tied all the ropes together," Young suggested, getting up to see for himself.

As he approached the window, he suddenly

stumbled and fell heavily against Chet. The chubby youth lost his balance and, with a yell, started to plunge over the sill!

Desperately Joe leaped forward and grabbed Chet's pants leg. He managed to hold on long enough for Frank to seize their friend's arm and clutch his shirt. Together the Hardys pulled him back into the loft.

Chet was as white as chalk and Joe's hands were shaking.

"I'm sorry!" Young said, staring at the boys. "I didn't mean to—it was an accident—I——"

Chet gulped. "That's okay, professor. It's just that I'm not built for flying." He tried a brave smile, and Young turned around in embarrassment to sit with Dr. Jenson.

The boys stood without talking for a while. Finally Frank said, "There's only one possibility and that is to clear the boarded-up windows. Maybe we can escape through one of them and climb down one of the other walls."

The young detectives wrenched the boards loose from each window, but were disappointed. The ground and the roof remained inaccessible.

"There goes our last chance," Joe said, discouraged. "We can't climb up or down, and the only stairs are guarded!"

Suddenly Frank had an idea. "Do you have a pencil?" he asked his brother and Chet.

"Yes, here," Joe said. "Why?"

Frank pulled a piece of paper out of his pocket and scribbled a hurried message. *"Help. We are being held prisoners in the warehouse!"* Then he leaned through the window and tossed the paper out. It drifted down onto the deserted street.

"Do you have any more paper?" Joe asked, excited.

"No. Do you?"

"No."

Chet did not have any either, and Frank said, "Let's ask the others."

The two scientists were involved in a serious conversation. Dr. Young had scribbled a number of equations on a piece of scrap. He looked up in surprise when the boys approached him. "This is all I had," he declared. "What do you need it for?"

They explained, and he said, "Forget it. This place is obviously so deserted that no one would find it anyway."

"It was a good try," Chet said. "And we have nothing to lose, right?"

"I suppose so," Young muttered, but he did not seem convinced.

They sat in silence for a while, overwhelmed by the hopelessness of their situation. Joe stared out the small window, his mind desperately trying to find a solution. Suddenly he sat up straight.

"Hey, did you see that?"

"See what?" Frank asked.

"The rope! In front of the window!"

"What?" Everyone looked in the direction of the opening, at the same time noticing a scuffling of feet on the roof.

"Someone's up there!" Frank exploded, as the rope came into view again, swinging back and forth wildly in the empty space.

"He's climbing down!" Joe shouted.

Young and Jenson stood up. They were about to rush to the window when a man shinnied down the rope, braced his foot against the wall, pushed back, and swung forward in a wide arc through the opening into the loft.

Everyone stared in amazement as the newcomer landed and bounced in an upright position. He looked at them with a big smile.

Jenson and Young hastened over, and Frank cried out, "Dad!"

"Mr. Hardy?" Chet mumbled, his mouth agape. "Is it really you?"

"Mr. Hardy!" Young stammered. "Are—are you here alone?"

"Yes," the detective replied, looking intensely at the scientist.

"Dad, how did you get here?" Joe asked. "We thought you were still in Florida at the Space Flight Center!"

"I discovered a clue that led me to Australia. Then I got a line on the gang ringleader. I followed him till I came to this place."

"Why did you post yourself on the roof?" Joe wanted to know.

"I knew the gang was using the warehouse as a hideout, and I had reason to expect them to bring you here. When they left this morning, I followed them but lost them. So I came back and decided to wait. I climbed up to the roof, tied a rope around the big weathervane, and eventually saw the gang taking you up to the loft."

"You think we'll get out of here safely?" Jenson asked anxiously.

Fenton Hardy nodded. "We will, except for the one rocket scientist who's at the bottom of this mystery."

Jenson turned pale. "I don't understand. Are you accusing me?"

"Not you, Dr. Jenson."

"Then what do you mean?"

Fenton Hardy looked straight at Young. "Professor, you're facing criminal charges in Australia and the United States!"

CHAPTER XX

Surprise in Port Augusta

As THE boys and Jenson stared in utter astonishment, Fenton Hardy pointed a finger at the professor. "You were behind the whole thing!"

"Prove it!" Young sneered.

"I will, and you'll spend time in prison! You're under arrest!"

"That's what you think, Hardy!" Young snapped viciously. "This is your last case. We've got you outnumbered. You're finished!" Pulling a whistle from his pocket, he blew a shrill blast that echoed through the whole building.

Bruno's voice responded from the landing at the top of the stairs. "Okay, chief," he said and turned the massive key in the lock. He pushed the door open and entered, covering the group with a revolver while Young moved over to join him.

Footsteps pounded up the stairs. Led by Stiller, the rest of the gang came in. The Cutlers brought up the rear with puzzled looks on their faces. "What's going on?" Cutler asked.

"We caught a real big fish this time," Young chuckled. He pointed to the Bayport detective and asked Stiller, "Do you know who this is?"

Stiller grinned. "Sure. That's the gumshoe Fenton Hardy, who sent me to jail ten years ago. I've been itching ever since to get even!"

"You were guilty," Mr. Hardy reminded him. "You got what you deserved."

Stiller scowled. "I'd have got away with it except for you. Now I'll take care of you and your punk sons, too."

"This is your chance for revenge," Young said. "Get them out of here. I don't want to see any of them again, ever!"

"It'll be a pleasure!" Stiller snarled.

He and his gang moved forward. Frank doubled his fists. "We may as well go down swinging!"

Joe assumed a karate stance with upraised palms and challenged the gang, "You won't take us without a fight!"

Stiller looked at Cutler. "Shall we finish them off here?" he asked roughly.

Cutler shook his head. "I had to rent this dump. Any evidence of a crime committed here might be traced to me. We'll take them to the woods out in back. There'll be plenty of cover out there."

Cutler glanced at Young. "Sure you've got all the dope you need from Jenson?"

Young nodded impatiently. "Don't worry about that. He's given me the final equations. Come on —let's finish this job so I can get back to Woomera."

The gang began to circle the boys and Mr. Hardy held up a hand. "Don't resist," he told the boys.

The advice surprised the three so much that the gang members were able to break through and overpower them after a brief struggle.

"Tie 'em up again and do a better job this time," Mrs. Cutler commanded as Bruno picked up the ropes and handcuffed the prisoners.

"Dad!" Frank cried out. "Why did you tell us not to fight?"

"There's no need to resist," Mr. Hardy said. "Didn't you hear tires screech down below?"

The gang froze in dismay, then Cutler dashed to the open window and looked down. "It's the cops!" he cried. "Let's get out of here!"

He and Mrs. Cutler ran from the loft and down the stairs, followed by other members of the gang. But the police already had the building surrounded. A detective sergeant and several uniformed constables arrested and disarmed the crooks as they tried to escape. The prisoners were herded back upstairs, and the captives were untied.

"You're right on time, sergeant." Fenton Hardy grinned.

"No trouble, sir. Mr. Moran alerted us a couple of hours ago."

"Mr. Moran?" Frank asked incredulously.

"That's correct," Mr. Hardy replied. "Here he comes." He pointed to Michael, who had followed the police to the loft.

Chet's mouth dropped open. "Mike! Wh-what are you doing here?"

"It's a long story," Mike said with a smile as the criminals were handcuffed and taken downstairs by the officers.

Professor Young stared at the newcomer. "You double-crossing rat!" he fumed. "You were supposed to be working for *us!*"

"Sorry, professor." Mike grinned coldly. "I happen to be working for the U.S. government. And it was my assignment to investigate the Cutler-Stiller gang for a series of international kidnappings and other offenses. I didn't know then they were behind the Jenson disappearance."

"Fantastic!" Frank exclaimed. "So you got a job with them—saying the law was after you?"

Mike grinned. "I'm sorry I couldn't tell you the truth, Frank. Now I can because my assignment is over and I'm a free agent again."

"What about Mr. Ponsley?" Chet asked.

"I had to let him know because I wasn't going with him."

"But how did you meet with Dad?" Joe inquired.

"After I left Ponsley at the airport, I phoned my superior at the U.S. Consulate," Mike went on. "He instructed me to assist Mr. Hardy in the Jenson case and the rounding up of the gang. So I met your father in Sydney and told him all I'd learned. We combined forces and flew into Port Augusta yesterday evening. By pooling all we knew, we were able to trace Stiller's mob to this warehouse—but we still didn't have the evidence to convict Young."

"You've got it now," said Chet. "Boy, what a case! So that's why you couldn't let your dad know what you were doing or where you were."

Mike nodded. "But it's all over now." He glanced at the two Hardy boys. "By the way, your deductions about that bank security guard were correct. Thurbow has confessed that he was the one who tipped off the robbers about the alarm system, and that he switched those chemicals in the hope of putting the Hardys out of action."

By now all the crooks had been taken downstairs except for Young. When a constable approached him with a pair of handcuffs, the scientist made a sudden break for the window. He squirmed through, grabbed the rope still dangling outside, and in seconds had shinnied down to the ground.

The constable leaned out the window and took aim with his gun.

"Don't shoot!" Mr. Hardy warned. "We want him alive!"

Frank edged past them and went down the rope after the fugitive. Young headed for the woods behind the warehouse, and Frank followed at top speed. Joe, meanwhile, flew down the stairs, hoping to head Young off. The others followed.

The prisoners were being loaded into police cars in front of the warehouse. The constable paused to explain the latest turn of events to the sergeant, while Mr. Hardy and Chet followed Joe around to the rear of the building, just in time to see Frank disappear into the woods.

"Young must be ahead of him!" Joe said as they hurried after the young detective.

Frank lost sight of Young among the trees, but a path led him through the underbrush and he went forward until he came to a fork, where he had to guess which way Young had gone. He decided to take the left branch. A hundred yards in he caught sight of the fugitive.

Young, glancing over his shoulder, noticed Frank. Puffing from exertion, he darted from the path into the underbrush. He stumbled and tripped in the thick shrubbery, but he refused to slow down because he could hear his pursuer forcing his way through after him.

Young reached the right-hand path, looked around, and then ran back toward the fork, hoping to confuse Frank.

Joe, meanwhile, had taken the right-hand path, his father and Chet the left. The boy ran until he reached a towering tree, where he paused to get his bearings. He heard a rustling sound and looked up.

Young leaped down on him!

The rocket scientist hit the younger Hardy between the shoulders, and the pair went down amid leaves, vines, and plants. Stunned by the collision, Joe felt Young's hand closing around his throat and choking off his breath. Grimly he struggled to break the hold. The man had a strategic advantage over him, and Joe gasped convulsively. The branches of the tree above him seemed to swing wildly as if whipped about by a heavy storm; then everything darkened and Joe went limp.

Suddenly he felt a hand pull him by the shoulder. He seized a wrist with his last bit of strength.

"Hold it," Frank said. "It's me!"

"Where's Young?" Joe croaked.

"He ran off when he saw me coming—back toward the warehouse. We've got to get him. Think you'll make it?"

"Sure, now that I can breathe again!" Joe rubbed his throat and the boys raced up the path. They reached the open space behind the warehouse and spotted Young jumping into the gang's pickup. Two policemen hurried around the corner, but Young got the truck going and roared straight at them, forcing them to spring out of the way.

The man powered toward a side road near where the Hardys emerged from the woods.

"Don't get in front of him!" Frank warned his brother. "He'll run you down!"

"I won't," Joe replied, "but this will! Give me a hand, Frank!"

Together, they levered up a fallen log from the ground and hurled it under the front wheels of the speeding truck. The vehicle struck the log with a thump, careened wildly to one side, and jolted to a halt in the underbrush.

The Hardys pounced on Young and dragged him out of the driver's seat. Realizing he could not escape again, he surrendered without a struggle. He too was loaded into one of the police cars in front of the warehouse, where Frank and Joe rejoined their father and Chet.

The Australian police detective complimented the Hardy boys on their quick thinking and fast action. "Now we have the whole gang," he added with satisfaction.

Young gave Fenton Hardy a venomous stare. "What made you suspect me?" he rasped.

"Frank and Joe asked me to check out Smoky Rinaldo. He'd found all the clues at the Aerospace Lab that seemed to incriminate Dr. Jenson, and he could easily have planted them himself. But he turned out to be clean, as far as I could tell. Then I realized you could have planted the clues just as easily. What's more, you were the only person who could have kept the gang tipped off about Frank and Joe's moves. For that matter, you were probably the one who stole that pass Stiller used to get into the Aerospace Lab."

"So Stiller followed us around the lab," Frank commented. "And, on orders from Young, he shadowed us at the Nassau Club."

Joe looked at Young. "You put on an act at the Princeton Library! You told me Stiller got out of the elevator and ran upstairs. Instead, you probably warned him to leave through the front door while you sent us on a wild-goose chase!"

Young glared at him but said nothing.

Frank spoke up. "And you told Stiller that we would be flying to Sydney so he could resume his job in Australia. By the way, was it you who phoned us at Sydney Airport and threatened us after we'd returned there with Mike Moran and Dr. Jenson?"

"What do *you* think?" Young snapped.

"I think he's right," Chet broke in. "I also think it was you who made that phone call to the hotel here in Port Augusta to keep Frank and Joe busy while your gang kidnapped Dr. Jenson from our room."

"Right," said Joe. "By that time, his private pilot was probably already flying back to Woomera to pick him up and bring him here."

"And later," Chet said to Young, "you tried to push me out of the warehouse window. If you weren't handcuffed, I'd punch you right in the nose!"

Dr. Jenson spoke up with indignation. "Arthur, why did you go through that miserable play acting up in the warehouse loft just now?"

"Because I needed the last Firebird equations you'd been working on. That's why. So I pumped you for the information in order to handle the project on my own."

"But I don't understand. Why was that so important to you?"

"I can answer that," Mr. Hardy said. "In case you didn't realize it, Young's been working for a foreign power. When their intelligence agents picked up news of the Firebird's development, they approached Young and paid him to eliminate you, Dr. Jenson, so *he* would be the one controlling the project. He was then to devise a scheme to foul up the launching in such a way that it would take NASA a long time to find out what went wrong. Young was supposed to turn over all our plans to this power so they could build a Firebird rocket of their own before we could recover from the foul-up and thus be ahead of us in this area of our space program."

Frank shook his head in disgust. "It's a good thing we prevented him from going through with his scheme," he said. Frank was proud that he had had a part in solving the case, but also felt the familiar emptiness he always experienced when a case was finished. Would there ever be another mystery for the Hardy boys? Frank did not realize at this moment that their help would soon be needed in *The Sting of the Scorpion.*

"Well, Dr. Jenson," Joe said, "now the tables are turned. You'll be in charge of the rocket launching."

"And it'll be right on schedule!" Chet added enthusiastically. "I'm sure it'll be a great success!"

Frank nudged his friend and grinned. "Not like yours at Bayport Meadow, Chet!"